Terri –
Plainridge,

God bless,
Stu

Plainridge

Romans
8:28

Steve Stratton

innovo
PUBLISHING

Published by
Innovo Publishing, LLC
www.innovopublishing.com
1-888-546-2111

Providing Full-Service Publishing Services for
Christian Authors, Artists & Organizations: Hardbacks, Paperbacks,
eBooks, Audiobooks, Music & Film

PLAINRIDGE

Library of Congress Control Number: 2013949053
ISBN 13: 978-1-61314-170-0

Cover Design & Interior Layout: Innovo Publishing, LLC

Printed in the United States of America
U.S. Printing History

First Edition: September 2013

To my Laura, all my love now and forever

2 November 1858

The stench from his bloated, decomposing corpse has traveled throughout the town. Yesterday, several women, including myself, approached Constable Brown and pleaded with him to cut Reverend Silas down, but he refused. He plainly stated that Hester Lynch would not allow it. I fear for what we have done. May God have mercy on us and our beloved town.

From the diary of Dorothy Lee
November 2, 1858

PROLOGUE

"SLOW DOWN, TOMMY!"
"Shut up! I don't wanna hear anything from you, Blake; this is all your fault."

"Why's it my fault? You wanna be on the lacrosse team just as bad as I do."

"It's your fault we're sleeping out in those woods tonight. It would've been easier to ding dong ditch Old Lady Crenshaw."

"Y'all both need to shut up," Scott Fisher abruptly yelled from the backseat. "We've already made our choice."

It was initiation night for the Plainridge Tigers lacrosse team. Each year, after fall tryouts, new members of the team are given their choice of two options, which they must select one and complete, in order to join the team. In past years, some of the options included catching and swallowing twenty squirming goldfish from a dirty bowl of water or sitting on a block of ice in the freezing cold for thirty minutes. However, this year those forms of hazing, having been frowned upon by local school officials, took a different path.

For this upcoming school year, the three new players were Tommy Calhoun, Blake Ledbetter, and Scott Fisher, and they were given the following options by team captain and senior Jeff Lowe:

A) Drive out to the Crenshaw house and "ding dong ditch the Crenshaw witch."

or

B) Spend the night in the woods off County Road 10.

Tommy Calhoun, a tall, muscular boy with long, blond hair and blue eyes was still fuming over the option chosen by Blake Ledbetter and Scott Fisher. Blake and Scott's friendship went all the way back to first grade at Plainridge Elementary. Blake, nicknamed "Ears," was a skinny kid who was constantly picked on because of his large nose and ears, which were accentuated due to his short haircut. Scott, on the other hand, was a short, quiet, stout kid who thrived both academically and athletically.

Being natives of Plainridge, both Blake Ledbetter and Scott Fisher were well aware of the stories regarding Old Lady Crenshaw and the Crenshaw place. For them, this was an easy choice.

"All I know is that I had plans with Anna Thompson tonight, but instead I gotta spend the night out in the woods with you two idiots. All we had to do was go knock on some old lady's door and run," said Tommy.

"Tommy," Blake began after a couple minutes of silence. "You didn't grow up here. Everybody knows the Crenshaw place is haunted. The last thing any of us wants is that old witch coming after us. It'll be safer camping in the woods."

"I hope you're right," Scott replied in a grim tone. "My grandfather wasn't too happy when I told him where we were going."

"Oooohh . . . " Blake snapped back in a smart aleck tone, mockingly waiving his hands in Scott's face. "You worried Loretta Sikes is gonna get ya?" Tommy and Blake broke out in laughter at that remark. "Dude, she's dead!"

"That's not what her husband thinks," Scott replied in calm voice, looking up and locking eyes with Blake. He'd thought about mentioning the wooden cross in his backpack, but decided against it. Promising to take the cross was the only way his grandfather would concede in allowing him to go on the trip.

"Yeah, well, my dad says that George Sikes is crazy," Blake said.

Tommy Calhoun eased his foot off the accelerator and slowly pulled his blue Ford Explorer off the side of the road and parked. "Is this it?" Scott asked.

"Yeah, Jeff gave me the exact miles and told me to look for the red flags tied to the barbed wire fence. He said, 'That's where y'all camp for the night.'"

"That moron and those other seniors are probably hiding out there somewhere waiting to scare us," Blake remarked, looking through the passenger window into the dark woods.

"Let's get out there, setup camp, and get a fire going," Scott said.

The boys decided to setup camp near the edge of the woods where they could still have a clear view of Tommy's SUV. It didn't take them long to gather firewood, start a fire, and get their tents up. The three tents were lined up next to each other, facing the dark road, with the quiet forest behind them. Even though all three fully expected Jeff Lowe and the other seniors to try and pull something, it didn't prevent them from falling asleep. They were exhausted after a long lacrosse practice earlier that afternoon.

Scott Fisher barely remembered falling in and out of consciousness once his head hit the pillow, but he was suddenly awakened at ten o'clock by the sound of twigs snapping just behind their tents. The campfire had burned out. Now there was only the deep darkness of night. He listened intently, trying not to move, while holding his cross in his left hand. Something told him this wasn't Jeff Lowe and the seniors. The sound of footsteps grew closer; he could see the lone figure's silhouette standing outside his tent. A couple of minutes passed. The sound of fallen leaves and twigs being crushed had stopped. There was nothing but the still silence of the forest. Scott's heart was racing; he was trying not to breathe loudly. Then he heard it—a blood-curdling scream from Tommy's tent.

Several minutes passed by as the three men stood in silence in the small den. Earl Smith ran his fingers compulsively through his thick, gray hair while he stared wide-eyed at the floor in disbelief, seemingly unaware of the hot coffee that continued to pour out of the shattered mug next to his foot. Greg Jones paced back and forth between the fireplace and the dark green sofa trying to somehow convince himself that this was just a bad dream and that he would wake up at any time. It all seemed surreal.

The three friends had decided to gather at Earl's to discuss the incident at the Lynch house one year ago. It was supposed to be a time of healing and moving forward. However, the warm conversation turned cold when Cory casually mentioned that George Sikes had been telling people that he had seen Loretta peering at him through his bedroom window. She had finally come home to him—the same wife who had presumably died a year ago.

Finally, it was the husky nineteen-year-old, Cory, who spoke first. "What do y'all think we should do?"

It had been less than an hour since Jeff Lowe had called Cory in a state of panic. He, along with several seniors, had gone out to the woods to prank the boys but discovered their campsite abandoned. According to Jeff, who was barely able to form a sentence, they'd found Tommy's Ford Explorer parked by the side of the road, but when they found their campsite, all three tents had been torn apart and scattered. There was no sign of the boys. All they found was a bloodstained sleeping bag and blood splattered up against a pine tree. The last part hit Cory and Greg hard.

"We need to call 9-1-1 and make sure it's been reported and that Sheriff Hayes knows about it. He'll probably want to create a search party. We need to start searching for those boys," Greg said.

"I'll call 9-1-1," Cory said, leaving the room.

Greg and Earl resumed the conversation.

"Greg, somethin' tells me it was her."

"Could've been a wild animal?"

"C'mon, do you really believe that?"

Greg shrugged, "No, just hoping," he responded solemnly.

"How could we've been so naïve?"

"I dunno," Greg responded, leaning against the mantel over the brick fireplace. "I guess we were just so exhausted and relieved to get it all behind us. Deep down, I knew something wasn't right when I saw the sheriff driving off with Loretta in his backseat. I mean, I remember thinking, *Why's he heading in the opposite direction of the hospital?*"

"I guess now we know why Loretta had a closed casket service. There was no body in that casket!" Earl replied, raising his raspy voice. "I remember thinking that was very odd, but I trusted the sheriff, and I didn't want to cross him."

Cory came back in. "What are you guys talking about?"

"Cory, I think we have every reason to believe that the horror we all experienced a year ago may not be over.

Do you remember Sheriff Hayes putting Loretta Sikes in the back of his patrol car as we were leaving?" Greg asked.

"Yeah."

"Well somethin' happened and only Sheriff Hayes knows the truth," Earl explained from his dark leather recliner.

"I remember we checked her neck for bite marks but didn't find anything." Greg continued his relentless pacing.

"We could've missed it. It was very dark in that house and by the time we finally got to the fence, we were all exhausted and frazzled, not to mention covered in blood and scared out of our wits!" Earl responded.

"I think we need to go see Sheriff Hayes. We need to know the truth," Greg replied. "Let's head out to County Road 10. I bet he's out there organizing a search party. Hopefully we can help. Cory and I know Tommy, Blake, and Scott."

***

Greg's cell phone rang just as he got into his tan hardtop jeep. It was Rachel. "Hey, honey, you still at Earl's?"

"Just leavin'."

"Have you heard about the missing high-school students?"

"Yeah, we're heading that way to see if we can help with the search."

"You sound worried."

"I am. I don't think this has anything to do with a lacrosse initiation."

"Those boys were in my second-period English class. Will you call me when you know something?"

"Of course. I love you."

"I love you too. Bye."

Greg wanted to tell Rachel everything he suspected, but he wanted some answers first. He was very protective of her, and he didn't want to frighten her unnecessarily. She was the best thing that had happened to him in years, and she was everything he had always wanted in a wife. In just a couple of months, they would finally be married.

Greg's thoughts immediately turned back to Loretta Sikes and the stories of her reported sightings. Anxiety mixed with fear seized him as he shifted his jeep into the next gear. *I can't believe this is happening again. We should've finished it last year.*

ONE

The bright blue flashing lights from the two parked police cars could be seen from miles away. Greg slowly approached the congested area. Sheriff Hayes and Deputy Sims were already on the scene. Greg came to a complete stop and rolled his window down to speak to the deputy who was standing in the middle of the road directing traffic. To his right, he saw several flashlights in and around the edge of the woods. The search had begun.

The skinny deputy, with his deep country accent, shined his flashlight directly into Greg's eyes then around the jeep to see who was inside. "Good evening, Deputy, y'all find anything?" Greg asked, using his hand to shield his eyes. Sims lowered his flashlight and adjusted his brown police hat.

"Naw, I think the sheriff's 'bout to call it off for the night and resume the search tomorrow."

"Do you mind if we have a word with him?" Greg asked. "We knew those boys well."

"Sure, just pull over to the side. He's over by the fence talkin' to that fella."

Greg pulled his jeep over into the grassy area along the side of the road and placed it in park. The three men got out. In the distance, they saw the sheriff who appeared to be in a heated conversation with a large, elderly man with a bushy, gray beard and red suspenders; the old man was holding a flashlight.

The early morning dew was already sticking to Greg's boots and jeans, causing them to become increasingly wet as he waded through the thick, knee-high grass toward the sheriff.

"Dan, there ain't nothin' else we can do tonight," Hayes said, raising his voice. "We'll start the search again in the mornin'."

"John, that's my grandson out there."

"I understand that, but it's too dark. I'm calling off the search."

The large man turned around with tears in his eyes and began making his way back toward his truck. "That's Dan Fisher, Scott's granddad," Cory whispered into Greg's ear.

"Sheriff!" Greg yelled, making his way closer. "Did y'all find anything?"

"Naw, it's too dark. We'll start back in the mornin', but it wouldn't surprise me if those boys don't show up at school tomorrow, talkin' 'bout how they fooled us all."

"Jeff Lowe said there was blood splattered everywhere."

The sheriff's facial expression turned somber. "Could've been a bear attack; we'll know more tomorrow," he said.

Greg could feel his cold gaze go right through him.

"John, you really believe that?" Earl abruptly asked.

John Hayes let out a loud sigh while rolling his eyes, "Earl, I don't have time to fool with you right now. It's best if you just drop it." With that, the sheriff turned around and began calling the search off.

Greg, Earl, and Cory stood around for several minutes watching the men filter out of the woods and back to their trucks. Greg leaned over and whispered, "Let's hang around and let everybody clear outta here. I wanna have a look at that campsite."

"Greg, I think that's a great idea," Earl responded.

The three men waited until the last truck had pulled away before grabbing a couple of flashlights out of Greg's jeep and making their way into the woods toward the campsite. Anxiety grew within them as they passed the barbed wire fence and walked deeper into the woods. Greg's stomach was in knots. It suddenly occurred to him that this was approximately the same place where they had entered the woods last year when going to the Lynch house. He wondered if Earl and Cory were having the same sense of dread and fear.

In approaching the grizzly crime scene, they noticed Sheriff Hayes had officially taped off the area in order to preserve any evidence. Greg ducked under the bright yellow police tape, which was connected between several pine trees, and began shining his flashlight around the small area. Careful not to touch anything, the three men walked around looking for any clues. The lingering smell of smoke from the dying campfire was still strong. Greg could still see traces of smoke rising from the last stick of charred wood. Jeff Lowe was right. The tents had been ravaged by something. It was clear this wasn't an initiation gone badly. This was an attack, but where were the bodies? *Shouldn't there be body parts around the crime scene?* Greg wondered. It was as if they had vanished. Over by the last tent, Greg and Earl stopped and froze in horror at the sight of dark red blood splattered across the ground and on the nearby pine tree. The reality began to kick in that the boys weren't alive. Greg felt a lump in his throat and began to get choked up.

"Greg, over here," Cory whispered. He was squatting down next to a demolished tent. Cory's eyes were fixated on an object next to a red backpack. It was a hand-sized wooden cross. "Do y'all see what I see?"

"Yeah," Greg replied, squatting next to Cory, scratching the whiskers on his chin.

"Why would someone bring a cross out in the woods?" Earl asked with one eyebrow raised.

"Good question. Is there a name on the backpack?"

Trying hard not to touch anything, Cory leaned forward, shined his light across the top, and read the name out loud. "Scott Fisher. That was his grandfather we saw talkin' to Sheriff Hayes."

"What do you think, Greg?" Earl asked.

"I'm thinking me and Cory need to go see Mr. Fisher tomorrow. I wonder if he knew his grandson had a cross with him," Greg said, reaching over and picking up the cross.

TWO

The next morning, Greg and Cory pulled into Dan Fisher's driveway. They could see the old man through the window sitting at his kitchen table staring into space. He appeared totally unaware of their arrival. Greg reached over and discreetly put the cross, which they had found the night before, in his brown denim jacket pocket before getting out of his jeep.

It took a couple of knocks on the front door before they heard Dan Fisher stumbling around inside. "Can I help you?" he asked, looking at them through his screen door.

"Mr. Fisher, my name is Greg Jones and this is . . ."

"I know Cory; he and my Scott were friends. You're the youth pastor at the church."

"Yes sir . . . I knew Scott too. I know this is a tough time for you, but we were wondering if we could ask you a few questions?"

"Sure, c'mon in. I'm waiting to hear from the sheriff on when the search is gonna resume. I should've never let him go, but he kept on begging. I knew how much being on that lacrosse team meant to him."

They followed Mr. Fisher into his small kitchen and took a seat at his square, wooden table. Greg reached into his jacket pocket and gently laid the cross on the table. "Mr. Fisher, we found this at the campsite last night; it was lying next to Scott's backpack. Do you know if it belonged to him?"

When he saw the cross, Dan Fisher reached into his pocket and pulled out a white handkerchief; his eyes began to well up. "I gave him that cross before he left. I made him promise me that he'd take with him."

"If you don't mind me asking, why'd you give your grandson a cross to take on a camping trip?" Greg asked, being somewhat coy. He was curious to see how Mr. Fisher would respond.

The large, old man sat there for a moment, wiped another tear out of his eye, and just stared at Greg. Several uncomfortable minutes passed. No one said a word. Greg could tell he'd hit a nerve, but he waited patiently for the old man to respond. "You of all people should know why," Dan finally said. "I know what y'all did up at the Lynch house last year. Then Sheriff Hayes having that phony closed casket funeral service for her, and George Sikes goin' around town talkin' 'bout seeing her. I've lived a long time, been here my whole life. I should've never let Scott go."

Greg and Cory thanked Mr. Fisher for his time and excused themselves out the door. Greg couldn't wait to get into his jeep and call Earl. "Hello," Earl answered.

"Earl, me and Cory just left Dan Fisher's place. He's the one who gave Scott the cross to take on the trip. He knows about Loretta."

"Greg, we need to go back and see the sheriff. We need to know what he did with her body."

"I agree. He'll be busy with the search today, so we'll head out to his house tonight and hopefully get some straight answers."

"Sounds good. In the meantime, I'm gonna do some more research on the history of vampires."

***

Greg and Cory met at Earl's house at 6:30 p.m. Earl had just finished some intensive research on the Internet and found some interesting, but troubling, information. He greeted the two men on his front porch with his arms crossed and eyeglasses perched on the edge of his nose.

"Well?" Greg asked, walking up the steps to his porch.

"I found some very interesting information, and I don't think it's a mistake that we're going to see the sheriff tonight," Earl said.

Greg walked over to the cluttered kitchen table and began looking at several articles that Earl had printed off. "First of all," Earl began, "there've been several documented cases of vampirism throughout the world. I'm sure y'all heard of Jamestown, Virginia, the first American colony founded in 1607?"

"Sure."

"Have you ever heard about the lost colony of Roanoke?"

Taking a seat at the table, both Greg and Cory simply shook their heads and listened to the seventy-three-year-old local historian. Cory sat across from Greg with both elbows on the table, his fist pressed against his cheeks. Earl continued.

"Well, it's one of the greatest mysteries in American history. In 1587, a guy by the name of John White, commissioned by Sir Walter Raleigh, led a group of about 120 colonists from England to the New World. They landed on Roanoke Island, just off the coast of North Carolina. Due to the harsh conditions and limited supplies, John White decided to sail back to England to resupply the colony. When he returned, three years later, he found the colony totally deserted. It was as if they had vanished into thin air.

"There's no evidence they'd left the colony. No bodies were ever found. Everything was left completely intact. The only clue we have is a strange word, CROATOAN, which was carved into a fence post on the outer wall of the settlement. On a nearby tree, outside the settlement, they found the letters CRO carved into the bark."

"What does Croatoan mean?" Cory asked.

"No one knows for sure, but there's a local Roanoke historian, Dr. James Donaldson, who claims that the word is from an ancient Saxon language meaning, 'vampire.' Some believe that the word translated from Saxon to Greek means *daimon* or 'demon' in modern English. He believes one of the colonists carved it into the fence post as a warning."

"What about Indians?" Greg abruptly asked. "How do they know the local Indian tribes weren't responsible for the missing colony?"

"Donaldson claims there's no evidence they were attacked by any of the tribes in that area. According to him, if they'd been attacked, there would've been clear evidence. There would've been bodies, arrowheads . . . the settlement would've been burned. Actually, he claims there's evidence that the local Indians kept their distance from the colony, which he points out as really strange."

"Hmmm . . .," Greg mumbled in deep thought, tapping his fingers across the table. "That's interesting, but I don't see the connection."

"Well, I'm not through yet," Earl continued. "Several years ago, this historian dug up the skeletal remains of a white man with an arrow through his heart, not far from the settlement. He claims the skull he excavated had unusually sharp fangs for a human being."

"So this guy, Donaldson, thinks a vampire was responsible for the disappearance of the Roanoke colony?"

"Yeah, that's his theory that vampires existed in Europe for centuries and migrated over with the early settlers to the New World."

"What do the other historians think?" Greg asked.

"Well, of course, they think he's crazy, but that's not all." Earl reached over and pulled another article from the stack of papers. "There's another particular case that occurred in Eastern Europe that sounds similar to Plainridge. In Poland, there was a small village in the northern part of the country that had lived in fear of vampires for many years. During the Cold War, Soviet troops would randomly vanish and despite search and rescue missions, no bodies were ever recovered. It got so bad that Soviet troops stationed there refused to venture outside the village. Here's the interesting part . . . y'all ready?" Earl paused, studying their faces. "Just outside the village, carved into a tree, was the word CROATOAN."

Exhibit A—Roanoke Historical Society

"Now, this is where the story gets even more interesting. Based on this article, a fella by the name of Vladimir Cruski, a local farmer, felt compelled to rid the village of this evil curse."

"Wow!" said Cory.

"Yeah, that's exactly what I thought as I was reading the story this morning. Hold on, there's more. Once he felt he had enough people in town committed to his cause, they went to an old abandoned farmhouse a few miles away and drove stakes through the hearts of five vampires. But as the article moves forward, it states that they made a crucial mistake. They didn't account for all the vampires. Sound familiar?"

"Unfortunately, very familiar. What happened next?" Greg asked.

"The two remaining vampires went into a rage and attacked the village. The first person they attacked was Vladimir."

"Does that mean that Loretta will be coming after us?" Cory asked with fear draped across his face.

"Not necessarily," Earl replied, removing his reading glasses from his face. "Remember, she was unconscious when we found her and really only started coming out of it when she was in the back of the sheriff's car. Also, she probably hadn't turned yet. One of the books lying around here stated that it usually takes twenty-four to forty-eight hours for a victim to turn into a vampire."

"Well, what's she been doin' this past year? I mean, how has she survived?" Cory asked in a frantic tone.

"She's probably lived in seclusion either in the graveyard or in the woods, seeking shelter from the sun during the day and surviving on the blood of animals at night," Earl responded in a matter-of-fact tone like a professor lecturing a class. "And now she's craving human blood, which would explain the attack last night."

"Exactly, Earl, that's why I think it's important for us to talk to Sheriff Hayes. He's the last person she remembers, and he's probably the first person she'd come after," Greg explained.

"Hmmm . . . I wonder what he did with her body?" Earl asked as he leaned back in the chair and stared at the ceiling with his hands folded behind his neck.

"That's one of the first questions I plan on asking him," Greg replied.

"Does he know we're coming by?" Earl asked.

"No, I decided it would be best if we came unannounced," Greg said.

"Well, this should be interesting."

THREE

Sheriff John Hayes lived in a large, white, colonial-style farmhouse just a few miles outside of Plainridge, just off County Road 10, only a mile from where the boys had camped. The house had been built by Dorothy Lee's father in the early 1800s and had been in the family ever since. The widower lived alone after his wife's passing two years earlier. Never able to have children of their own, John was crushed when his wife, Emily, died. Many of his close friends thought that ever since then, John had become reclusive and bitter. Even the residents could tell that the sheriff was no longer the friendly, approachable man they once knew.

***

Fog covered the dark two-lane road causing Earl to keep his lights on dim and go slower than normal. Cory let out a couple of deep sighs as he looked at the creepy, low-hanging fog descending on the cornfields like an army of ghosts. After an uncomfortable fifteen minutes of silence, Earl decided to speak up. "There's one more thing I forgot to mention from the article, and it might be the most important of all."

"What's that?" Greg asked.

"At the conclusion of the article, the author suggested that there might've been a spiritual link or root cause as to why vampirism could've appeared in Poland. It's just speculation, but after World War II, the Soviets came in and established communism not only as the official government, but as the main religion. The Soviets were ruthless in persecuting the church. Basically, they asked God to leave."

Earl slowed down and turned off County Road 10 onto a one-lane dirt road that would take them to the Hayes' farmhouse. The narrow, winding dirt road ran parallel against a rusty barbed-wire fence all the way up to the house. The sound of dirt and gravel churning on the wheels soon gave way to the barking dog signaling a guest was arriving. Immediately, the outside lights on the house lit up the darkness. Earl placed the gearshift in park, and the three men piled out.

John Hayes stood on his large front porch, still in his tan uniform, arms crossed, and leaning up against a white column. He had a suspicious, but intense look on his face. "Little late for a visit, ain't it?" the sheriff shouted.

"Sorry to pop in so late, Sheriff, but I think this is important," Earl hollered back. "It has to do with the missing boys."

"C'mon in; just me and Butch here anyway."

Cory stared at the muscular, black pit bull, who was in alert mode and seemed none too happy to have unannounced guests.

"What can I do for you boys tonight? Must be important if it can't wait till mornin'."

John Hayes made his way into the den and collapsed into his favorite chair. Greg glanced around and noticed that the place was incredibly filthy. Papers and clothes were scattered across the floor along with spilled dog food. Flies swarmed over a sandwich that looked like it had been lying on the kitchen table for days, and there seemed to be a horrible odor coming from the kitchen. Greg assumed it was old trash that needed to be taken out.

"Sheriff, it's been almost a year since our episode at the Lynch house," Earl began.

"Is that why y'all came out here? I thought I told y'all not another word about that night." The sheriff leaned over to spit tobacco juice into a large plastic jug next to his chair.

"I realize that, but I think you could be in grave danger."

"What in the Sam Hill are you talkin' 'bout, Earl?"

"Sir, my name is Cory Reynolds and . . ."

"I know who you are."

"Well sir, there are these kids at school, who live close to Mr. Sikes, and they said he's been tellin' folks that he's seen Loretta."

"I know all 'bout that. Poor George Sikes has lost his mind if you ask me," the sheriff replied.

"Are you sure about that, John?" Earl inquired.

"Heck yeah, I'm sure of it. Now, I don't want y'all digging into this anymore. Do you hear me? I don't need it and the town don't need it, especially right now."

"Anything new on the search for the missing boys?" Greg asked.

"Nope, and it don't look good. I'm leaning toward a bear attack, but we'll continue searching."

"Sheriff, are bear attacks common in this area?" That question didn't a get a response, only an icy stare. Earl continued to press the issue. "Sheriff, is it possible that if there was a bear attack there'd be body parts left at the scene?" Earl was walking on thin ice. Hayes didn't respond to the question but continued to give him an angry look.

"Can I just ask one more question, and then we'll leave," Earl pressed.

"What?"

"Sheriff, what'd you do with Loretta's body?"

The sheriff's blood began to boil. Earl had crossed a line, and he instantly knew it. John Hayes' head turned beet red. He rapidly rose out of his chair and made his way over to Earl. Earl, Greg, and Cory immediately started backing up toward the front door.

"GIT OUT!" John Hayes shouted, pointing to the door. Butch stood up and growled as the situation began to quickly deteriorate.

"John, please, we just need to know, that's all," Earl said in a pleading tone, his hands raised in a self-defense posture.

"I SAID GIT OUT!"

"Sheriff, if she's alive, she may be coming after you!" Greg stated emphatically, positioning himself between Earl and the sheriff.

That piece of information stopped him in his tracks. Greg continued.

"John," he spoke in a softer, more personal tone, trying to lower the tension in the room. "It's not too late to turn to God."

"God?" John Hayes responded with his eyebrows raised in surprise. "Where was 'God' when I watched my friends get blown to pieces in Vietnam?" He continued. All the pent-up hurt and pain seemed to be coming out at once. "Where was your 'God' when I watched my wife die a slow, painful death as cancer ate through her body?"

"John, I don't have the answers to your questions, but I know what it's like to lose someone close, and I know He's there to comfort us and walk with us through the pain," Greg responded with sympathy. "You know, you can't blame God for all the evil in the world. There's an enemy—"

John interrupted, "Well, if that works for ya, then fine, but I don't need that kinda God. So, for the last time, get out of my house."

"Sheriff, please just tell us what you did with her body. I promise we won't say a word. If she was really bitten, then there's a chance she could've become a vampire," Greg pleaded.

"You boys still think I'm stupid, don't ya. Why do you think I told you to put her in my patrol car in the first place?" No one answered. They just looked at each other. The sheriff continued. "Because I didn't want to take any chances in case she'd been bitten . . . that's why."

"John, what did you do with her? Please tell us," Greg pleaded once again.

"Aight, if it'll shut you up and get you out of here, I'll tell you. I didn't feel a pulse, so to be on the safe side, I drove her to Asbury Cemetery and buried her in a grave in the back. I made up the story about her getting hit by a car for George and the town.

"I convinced George that her body had been torn up pretty bad and that he didn't want to see her like that. It was best for everyone to have a closed-casket service. There you have it. Case closed!"

"John, I hate to tell you this, but based on some of our research, vampires can only be killed by either driving a stake through their heart or setting them on fire," Earl hesitantly responded, expecting the worst.

"Oh is that a fact?" Hayes responded sarcastically while folding his arms and tilting his head in a condescending manner. "I'll tell you what, I've seen a lot of things in my life, but I ain't ever seen anybody or anything climb out of five feet of dirt. Good night!"

***

Greg drove Earl's truck back to town. The old man was visibly exhausted after the heated exchange with John Hayes. The fog was thicker now than when they had first arrived at his house.

"I don't understand why the sheriff got so angry?" Greg asked.

"Greg, it's like I told you last year. A lot of folks in Plainridge don't like talking about the town's history, especially the older folks. The stories about people suddenly disappearing, never to be seen again, have been secretly passed down through the generations. Our town's got a dark past and people are afraid that if it's talked about, it'll come back. I think John's mainly concerned about keeping outsiders away because that's what the town wants him to do."

"But I just don't understand . . ." Greg was about ramble on.

"AHHHHH! GREG, LOOK OUT!" Earl screamed, pointing toward the road. He felt the seatbelt suddenly tighten across his chest, slamming him back into the seat.

Greg jerked the stirring wheel sharply to the left, causing the truck to swerve, as he dodged a white object darting across the road. After regaining control, Greg swiftly pulled the truck back onto the right side of the road and came to a complete stop.

"What was that?" Greg asked.

Earl and Cory were strangely silent. Only the sound of their labored breathing filled the air.

"Greg, did you see that?" Cory asked.

"All I saw was a white blur darting across the road."

"I think I saw her," Earl replied, with a look of terror across his face. He looked intently outside the passenger window into the open fields.

"Loretta?" Greg asked.

"Yeah . . . I'm . . . I'm sure it was her. In an instant, I saw a woman in white with ghostly skin and long, black hair looking at us through the fog," Earl stammered.

"I saw it too," Cory replied. "Her face was evil."

"What if she's headed to John's house? We've gotta warn him. Do you know his number?" Earl asked.

"No, but I'll call 9-1-1. They'll put me through to him," Greg said. He dialed the number on his cell phone.

"9-1-1 operator, how may I assist you?"

"I need to speak to Sheriff Hayes," Greg replied frantically. "Can you transfer me to him?"

"Sir, is this an emergency?"

"Uh . . . well . . . uh . . . maybe?" Greg said, not really knowing what to say. Several seconds of complete silence went by as Greg searched his brain for something to tell the operator. He was drawing a complete blank. *Think Greg!*

"Sir, may I remind you that this line is for emergencies only. Any violation could result in harm to others and constitute a criminal offense. Good night."

"What do we do now?" Cory asked.

"I'll look his number up at home and give 'im a call," Earl replied. "That's the only thing we can do now. Going back to his house could be a fatal mistake."

FOUR

Still in his tan uniform, the overweight, aging sheriff found himself in his typical nightly routine, sound asleep in his La-Z-Boy recliner. It had been a couple of years since John Hayes had slept in his bed. After the passing of his wife, he rarely even went into their bedroom. The pain was still too great.

The only sound that resonated through the empty house was John's snoring, which never seemed to bother Butch. Each night the faithful pit bull curled up on the cold floor next to his master's chair. This night, however, was different. John was suddenly awakened by Butch growling and barking at the front door. Startled and confused, he slowly roused himself from the chair. Still rubbing his eyes, his confusion turned to anger. "What is it, boy?" he asked, looking down at his loyal companion. "Earl Smith, I've had just about enough of you and your friends. I've given you my last warning." By now, Butch was attacking the door with both paws and barking madly as the black fur on his back stood straight up. John had never seen the dog act in this way before. His law enforcement instincts began kicking into full gear. "Sick 'em, boy," he said, cracking open the front door. Butch almost knocked him down as he shot out the door to confront the intruder.

The next sound he heard was his strong pit bull whimpering and then silence. Scared and confused, John Hayes quickly walked back into the den, grabbed his shotgun from his gun cabinet, and began loading it. He sensed that something was very wrong and that this was not Earl, Greg, and Cory back for another visit. He turned on the front porch lights and carefully looked out the window before heading out to find Butch.

With his heart racing, he reached down to open the front door, but a strange sound on the window along the right side of the house caught his attention. It was a soft tapping on the window, followed by a long, high-pitch scraping sound, like when someone runs his fingernail across a blackboard. He wondered if it was merely the wind causing a branch to gently bump up against the house. The sheriff cocked his shotgun and slowly walked over to the window. The tapping continued. *Tap . . . Tap . . . Tap. . . .* It sounded like someone with a long fingernail was gently tapping the window as if he wanted in.

As a young man, John Hayes did two tours of duty in Vietnam and witnessed all the horrors that war could offer. Needless to say, he was rarely frightened, but in this case, he found himself shaking as he lifted his shotgun up to the window.

With one hand he reached for the curtain and, in one swift motion, pulled it back. He suddenly found himself face to face with Loretta Sikes. Her face was filled with malice and hatred. He screamed when her cold, pale hands shattered the window and grabbed his throat. The vampire jerked the large man through the window with ease as she continued to clutch his throat. Large amounts of dark red blood poured from the deep lacerations across his head and face, dripping onto the vampire's pale hand and onto his uniform. Bloodied beyond recognition, he struggled for his life.

He desperately tried to remove her hand. "Please . . ." was the last word John ever spoke. Loretta had crushed his esophagus.

***

Later that night, as Greg sat close to Rachel, his mind kept drifting back to the chaotic scene at the sheriff's house and the utter terror of seeing Loretta Sikes' ghostly figure crossing the road in front of them.

"Greg, are you okay? You haven't said two words since you've been here."

"Yeah, I'm okay. Sorry honey, I guess I've got a lot on my mind."

"Thinking about those missing boys?" Rachel asked.

"Yeah, I'm afraid it doesn't look good."

"A lot of students were upset today. During the morning announcements, Principal Morgan encouraged all the students to talk to the school's counselor if they need to and to keep the boys and their families in their thoughts and prayers."

"Hey, do you have a cross in the house?" Greg suddenly asked.

"Of course, but why do you ask?"

Rachel knew about Greg's experience last October. He had decided early in their relationship to share with her the events that had occurred at the Lynch house. Even though she wasn't sure if she totally believed the story about vampires in Plainridge, she knew Greg had been deeply affected by something he had encountered on that fateful night. She loved this man and wanted to spend the rest of her life with him. Greg had been the type of man she had prayed for all of her life. Unlike most of the people in town, Rachel Stone was not a native of Plainridge. Like Greg, moving here was the last thing she wanted to do after graduation. She only reluctantly took the teaching job at Plainridge High School because it was the only job available. She remembered how lonely she felt when she first arrived in town and the weird stares from people as she walked down Main Street. It was as if they were saying, "Who are you and why are you here?" Going to church, sitting in a near-empty pew, and then coming home to no one was difficult.

There were so many times she had considered just packing up and leaving, but then one day Cory Reynolds approached her and mentioned that he would like to introduce her to his friend Greg. The rest was history. She briefly reflected back to the introduction at the school Christmas party. At first, Greg seemed shy, but as she looked into his big, brown eyes, she saw a kindness mixed with a deep pain. She knew that feeling too.

After several minutes of continued silence, Rachel decided to work up enough courage to ask him about last October. "Honey, do you mind if I ask you a question?"

Greg turned his head, gently smiled at his beautiful fiancée, and slowly began to caress her long, black hair. He loved looking into her eyes. Her deep brown eyes seemed to go on forever. "Sure honey, you can ask me anything."

"Did something happen tonight at Earl's house? I mean, I know it's been a year since the incident at the Lynch house and with you asking me about having a cross and all . . ."

Even though Greg wanted to protect Rachel, he knew he should go ahead and tell her about Loretta. "Rach, do you remember me telling you how we found Loretta Sikes in the cellar at the Lynch house and how Sheriff Hayes told us to put her in the backseat of his patrol car?"

"Yeah, I think I remember you telling me about that," Rachel replied.

"Well, I know this might sound crazy, but we think Loretta may still be alive."

"What do you mean alive? I thought you said they had a funeral for her."

"They did and the whole town turned out. It was a couple of weeks before you moved here. It was a closed casket service. We all thought it was over," Greg replied.

"Greg, you're not any making sense. How can she still be alive?"

"Her husband, George, has been telling folks that he saw her outside his bedroom window. Then there was the unexplained attack last night not far from the Lynch house.

It's not outside the realm of possibility that she was bitten and is now a vampire. I realize that may be hard to accept and I wouldn't believe it either, if I hadn't seen it with my own eyes. Also, we went to Sheriff Hayes' house tonight to find out what exactly happened and what he did with her body."

"What did the sheriff say?" Rachel asked.

"You mean before he threw us out of his house?" Greg chuckled. "He said that he buried her in a grave in the back of Asbury Cemetery. The problem is that we think we saw her crossing County Road 10 tonight on our way back to town. As a matter of fact, I think I almost hit her."

"Greg, do you think it could've been your imagination or an animal crossing the road?"

"I don't think so because Earl and Cory said they saw her face up close."

Rachel got up off the couch, walked over to her desk, and began digging in one of the drawers.

"What are you looking for?" Greg asked.

"I have an old church directory around here somewhere. My friend Lisa gave it to me. I bet Loretta's picture is in it," Rachel replied, continuing to rummage feverishly through the drawers. "Found it."

Rachel went back to the couch and sat down next to Greg. They scrolled through the church directory, which was in alphabetical order. "Reynolds, Ritz, Schultz, Sikes. Here she is."

A brief moment of awkward silence filled the air. There was nothing but the sound of the clock ticking over the mantle. Rachel felt chill bumps rising up her arm and the back of her neck. "Greg, do you think she looks a lot like me? I mean, I could pass for her daughter."

Greg was speechless. He couldn't stop staring at the photo. His mind flashed back to the encounter earlier that evening on County Road 10. In an instant, he remembered her ghostly face through the fog. *She wasn't dead or was she?* "Yeah, you're right. Y'all do favor a lot."

"Honey, this gives me the creeps."

"Rach, I know this probably sounds silly, but it would make me feel better if you put a cross on your door. At least until we can get some answers."

"Okay, I think I'd feel better too," she said, gripping his hand tightly. "You can use the one that's on my dining room wall."

Greg held the brown wooden cross in his left hand as he hammered the nail through it and into the front door of Rachel's house. He was startled at the sound of a garbage can crashing in the alley behind him. *Probably just a cat*, he thought, looking intently down the narrow alley that joined Rachel's small one-bedroom home. In the distance, ominous flashes of lightning and thunder caught his attention, warning him that a storm was fast approaching. When he was finished, he kissed Rachel goodnight and headed back to his house. He prayed, "Lord, please keep her safe; she's all I got now."

FIVE

OCTOBER 28TH

E arly the next morning, Greg called Earl to see if he had been able to reach Sheriff Hayes. The phone rang three times before Earl's familiar deep, gravelly voice answered. "Hello?"

"Good morning, Earl. It's me, Greg. Just wondering if you were able to get a hold of the sheriff last night?"

"No, there was no answer. I thought about calling Deputy Sims, but decided not to."

"I wonder if he's made it in to work," Greg asked.

"I'll call the police station and see if he's made it in this morning. Then I'll meet y'all at Dot's for breakfast."

***

With the emergence of dawn, the early morning rain had finally stopped and now the cold north wind began to blow through the small town. Greg Jones turned onto Main Street and pulled his jeep into a small parking place next to Dot's diner; he noticed that Earl's truck was already there. Downtown Plainridge resembled most small Southern towns, with a large, white antebellum-style courthouse located in the center of the town square. Connected by a series of cracked sidewalks and two four-way stops, the courthouse was surrounded by various stores, including the local five-and-dime and traditional barber shop with its vintage red, white, and blue poles revolving out front. Like many towns scattered across the South, Plainridge was one of those places that time had forgotten.

Greg was greeted by a stiff autumn wind as he reached into his pockets for some change for the parking meter. His attention was subtly drawn to a large figure in the window next to Dot's. Jane's discount store was announcing their Halloween sale. The sign across the front door read: *Costumes & Decorations, 50% off.* Greg casually made his way over to the store and took a closer look at the mannequin in the front window. The tall figure was draped in a black cape and wore a ghostly white mask. The face looked eerily familiar, ushering in a flood of bad memories he had tried desperately to suppress. He stood there momentarily, mesmerized, with his hands in his pockets, studying the figure's white face and red eyes. Chill bumps slowly rose up his spine.

Interesting, he thought. A strong breeze sent a fresh set of autumn leaves down the shaded sidewalk, suddenly waking him from the trance he found himself in.

He walked into Dot's and saw Earl and Cory sitting in a booth in the back talking. Just above him on the mounted television was a female reporter from Channel 6 News out of Montgomery, wrapped up in a long, gray trench coat and microphone in hand. He immediately recognized that she was reporting from County Road 10, exactly where the search had begun a couple of nights ago. Behind her, he could see a few trucks parked along the side of the road.

Greg stopped to watch the broadcast and remembered this time last year when he couldn't sleep and decided to come down to Dot's for an early breakfast. He had found Cory and his friends sitting in the same booth. Reflecting back to that fateful morning it occurred to him it was not a coincidence that he had awakened at 3:30 a.m. He distinctly remembered Cory telling him that was the same time the boys were up at the old Lynch house.

"Good morning, guys," Greg said in a low, somber tone. He slid into the old, red vinyl booth next to Cory and across from Earl.

"Shhh," Earl replied, pressing his finger against his lips. "Hey Dot, you mind turning that up?" Earl yelled from the booth.

Dot grabbed the black remote from behind the cash register and aimed it up toward the TV as everyone in the restaurant listened intently.

"Abby, what's the latest on the missing Plainridge teenagers?" the news anchor asked the reporter.

"Mark, I haven't seen Sheriff John Hayes, who is leading the search, but I was able to talk to his deputy, Deputy Sims, from the Plainridge Police Department. According to the deputy, the boys were camping out in the woods behind me two nights ago. As of right now, the three teenage boys remain missing while the search and investigation goes on."

"Any reason for why the teenagers were camping out on a week night?" the anchor asked.

"Mark, apparently it was part of a lacrosse initiation. Interestingly enough though, this is not the first time this small town has had to endure this type of tragedy. If you remember, it was this time last year we were broadcasting from the same location about the missing woman, Loretta Sikes, who was later found dead. It was later confirmed by Sheriff Hayes that she had been killed in a hit-and-run accident."

"Abby, stay warm and please let us know if anything breaks in this story," said the handsome anchor before he began reading the rest of the news. Dot immediately grabbed the remote and turned the volume down.

"Did you sleep last night?" Cory asked.

"Not really," Greg replied. "I was up most of the night wondering if we did the right thing by not going back to the sheriff's house."

"I know me and the sheriff didn't see eye to eye on a lot things," Earl stated, while slowly stirring his coffee, "but something ain't right. I called his house several times last night, but there was no answer. I called the police station this morning, and they said he hadn't made it in yet and they hadn't heard from him. His assistant, Susie Price, told me that wasn't like him. He always came in early, before anyone else arrived, and made a fresh pot of coffee. I think something's wrong, but what could we have done? He threw us off his property!" Earl rambled on. He placed his elbows on the wobbly vinyl table and his hands on over his old, wrinkled face, concealing his guilt and grief.

"Why don't we just go back out there?" Cory whispered.

"I think you're right, Cory, we just need to go back and check on Sheriff Hayes. What's the worst thing he can do? Arrest us?" Greg asked in a rhetorical tone.

Earl thought about it long and hard, while softly scratching his white goatee. "You're right. Let's finish up breakfast and head that way."

***

Greg slowly turned onto the rough dirt driveway leading toward John Hayes' house, which sat on top of a hill like a small fortress. *No one's gonna sneak up on him*, Greg thought, studying each side of the old, white house. Not knowing what to expect, all three men stared anxiously at the house from inside the truck. It seemed like an eternity before Greg decided to make the first move. Earl was especially nervous. It had been less than twenty-four hours since his last confrontation with the sheriff. However, deep down, something told him there would be no confrontation this time.

All three men slowly crawled out of the truck and looked around before walking toward the wrap-around front porch. Greg was concerned about running into Butch, but thought it was odd that they hadn't seen or heard from the pit bull. Greg knocked loudly on the front door several times while Cory tried looking into the dirty, grimy windows.

"Let's walk around the side of the house. I can't believe we haven't heard from the dog," Earl said. Truthfully, Earl wasn't surprised at all and neither was Greg, even though both were silently committed to playing out this charade. That is, until they turned the corner of the wrap-around porch and found the gruesome sight of the sheriff's body. He was lying on his back across the porch; his head was turned sideways toward the men. All color and life was drained from his face. His mouth was wide open, and his pale face displayed a look of shock. Dried blood soaked through his tan uniform, causing the top portion of the uniform to become a maroon color. It appeared that his neck had been ravaged by some type of animal.

No one let out a scream, but they froze in horror at the sight of his rigid body. His vacant, cold eyes stared back at them. Earl immediately fell to his knees. He steadied himself against a white column on the porch. Cory leaned down to console the old man while Greg made his way over to the body. "Looks like he was jerked through this window," Greg said, squatting over the corpse.

"Don't touch anything, Greg. The last thing we need is our fingerprints on his body."

"What y'all think we should do?" Cory asked frantically.

"I suppose we should call the deputy and report a crime," Greg said.

"What crime?" Earl replied. "Oh you mean, a vampire wanted for murder? You should know by now, that's not what anyone in this town wants to hear."

"Well, what should we do?" Greg asked. "Should we drive a stake in his heart? What if he resurrects as a vampire?"

"I don't think that'll be necessary," said Earl. "It doesn't look like he was bitten. It looks more like a murder. This was vengeance. Just leave 'im here. Eventually, Deputy Sims will drive out here looking for him, and he'll find the body. At that point, he'll call Mayor Watson. I know both men well; I went to school with Ed. I guarantee you; they'll not want any outsiders involved. They'll declare it an accident and bury him at Asbury. Case closed and that's all they want."

"Guess you're right," Greg replied. "Sometimes I still forget about our town's culture."

"Unfortunately, that's the way it's always been," Earl replied, slowly gathering his composure while using the front column to pull himself up off the porch. He casually walked over to Greg and gently put his hand on his shoulder. "Speaking of Asbury, I say we head over to the cemetery. There's nothing more we can do here. I wanna have a look at Loretta's grave. She has to be hiding somewhere. Maybe we can catch her sleeping and end this now."

SIX

Asbury Cemetery was located on top of a hill on the opposite side of town from County Road 10. The top of the cemetery provided a panoramic view of the entire town. The large, Gothic stone crosses on the south end of town could be seen clearly from the top of the cemetery. Unless there was a football game or school event, most people never came to this end of town and considered it the long way to get to County Road 10 and out of Plainridge.

Surrounded by several pine trees, the old cemetery always had more than enough shade, which made it seem darker even during the mid-part of the day. The winds seemed to pick up as Earl's truck churned its way up the steep hill and through the open medieval cast-iron gate that bore the name ASBURY across the top. For years, the original cemetery was located behind the small, white church, but when the war started and a large number of dead bodies began arriving weekly by train, it was decided to relocate the cemetery to a hill at the north end of town. The only thing that remained were the two large, stone crosses, which were later moved to the edge of town.

Inside the rugged, unkempt cemetery, one main dirt road separated the graveyard into two halves. Earl followed the main road until it came to a dead end. "This cemetery's old; the graves here go back to the 1800s. Everyone that's ever lived in Plainridge has been buried here. Some of the oldest graves are in the very back. That's where the sheriff said he buried Loretta," Earl said. The old man got out of his parked truck and after surveying the area for a moment, like a dog trying to pick up a trail, he instinctively began walking to the left-hand side of the graveyard. "It's been a long time since I've been out here," he mumbled to himself.

Instead of following Earl, Greg pulled his red hoody over his head and casually wandered over to the right-hand side of the hill. He buried his hands into the pockets of his sweatshirt and took a moment to gaze at his hometown below. Standing underneath the shade of a large pine tree, his eyes easily located the town's famous stone crosses, and from there he followed Taylor Street all the way up the hill to Asbury. The school and adjacent football field was at the foot of the hill. One street over from Taylor was Main Street where he could clearly see the white courthouse. He took a few steps to his right and found the church. The large oak tree next to the church, which was the oldest tree in town, was now fully decorated in its autumn glory. The south part of town, past Main Street, was a cluster of small houses where most of the residents lived.

The last time Greg was here it was for his parents' funeral over five years ago. Their graves were located at the front of the cemetery. There wouldn't be time for a visit today. *Don't know if I'm ready for that yet,* he thought to himself.

"Greg, you comin'?" Earl hollered.

"Yeah," Greg replied, running to catch up with Earl and Cory.

The sun tried desperately to shine through the pine trees as the three men made their way through the countless headstones. Pine needles, fallen leaves, and overgrown brush covered most of the ground. It was apparent that the cemetery rarely had any visitors. Greg wondered if there was even a groundskeeper, considering the condition of the cemetery. Knee-high grass discreetly hid the names and dates on several of the tombstones. The lack of sunshine and brisk autumn breeze reminded Greg of last October. He felt the same anxious feeling growing in the pit of his stomach.

"This place is every bit as creepy as the Lynch graveyard," Cory said.

"John was smart burying her back here. All the new graves are up front; no one comes back here anymore," Earl replied, glancing over his shoulder at Greg and Cory. The old man was talking loudly. It was obvious he wasn't concerned about being heard. "Only problem is you can't bury vampires alive. They don't need oxygen to live, they have superhuman strength, and can certainly crawl out of a few feet of dirt."

"Why are we here then?" Cory asked with quizzical look on his face. "I mean, we know she's the one who got the sheriff and the three students, and with George Sikes tellin' folks he's seen her and all."

"That's a good question, Cory. I don't have any doubt that she escaped from the grave, but I think it's a good idea that we at least check it out," Earl replied.

Earl stopped near the back of the cemetery and began looking around for the grave.

"Over here," Greg motioned. "I found it. The sheriff even went as far as to put a headstone on her grave. Loretta Sikes 1960–2010 RIP."

Earl and Cory walked over to the very last grave where Greg was squatting, examining the excavated dirt. The wind had blown several blood red leaves up against the dingy, white headstone. Greg stared at the leaves and for a brief moment pondered the irony of the situation. "You think George Sikes ever comes out here to visit her grave?"

"Nope, he's told several people in town he could never bring himself to come out to Asbury. Heck, there wasn't even a graveside service," Earl confidently replied.

Earl looked suspiciously at the large hole at the top of the grave. Large amounts of dislodged red dirt had been cast to the side in every direction. It was obvious that either someone had dug down into the grave or Loretta had dug herself out. Greg looked down into the grave and could see her coffin at the bottom. It was closed with loose, brown dirt covering the top. His left hand began to shake uncontrollably at the thought of climbing down into the dark hole and opening her coffin.

"Think she's still in there?" Greg asked, his voice quivering.

"Only one way to find out," Earl replied. "Cory, if you don't mind, would you go back to my truck and fetch a few things?"

"Sure, what do you need?"

Loretta's Headstone

"In the back, there's a wooden stake, a hammer, a shovel, and a cross."

"I'll be right back."

Cory walked back to the truck to gather the items. Earl squatted down next to Greg and looked down into the hole. "Greg, this may be our chance to end it all. She's probably in there, sleeping."

"I don't know how I feel about driving a stake into her heart. What if she's really dead and we're wrong about her being a vampire?"

"Greg, you know deep down we're not wrong. Besides, if she's dead, what difference will it make? We'll just cover her grave back up and be on our way. Just think about it; do you really think somebody came out here and dug up her grave?"

"No, doesn't look like anybody's been back here in a long time."

"Exactly," replied Earl.

Both men looked up when they heard Cory approaching with the items in his hand. Greg grabbed the shovel and began moving more dirt from the grave. Bad memories flooded his mind. He never thought he'd be doing this again. It seemed like just yesterday that he, Earl, and Cory were digging up the Lynch graves. It's funny how certain smells, like the smell of the moist, deep earth, can trigger a person's deepest emotions. With every shovel load, Greg's fear grew. He wondered if Earl and Cory were having the same feeling. No one talked. Greg began to feel sick to his stomach.

"Okay Greg, I think you can get down there now," Earl said, looking down into the grave. He handed Greg the wooden stake and hammer. Greg Jones let out a loud sigh as he looked down at the coffin. In his mind he prayed, *Lord, please give me courage.*

Mysteriously, the winds began to pick up. The once bright, sunny sky was now covered by dark, rolling clouds. Greg gently lowered himself into the grave until he straddled the coffin. Moments seemed like an eternity as he stared at the latch that opened the top part of the coffin.

"Greg, hurry up!" Earl screamed. The wind began to blow even harder. Earl and Cory braced themselves against a large pine tree to keep the ferocious winds from blowing them away. Greg looked up and saw that the old man was genuinely frightened. Even though it was still in the early afternoon, the combination of the swaying pine trees and dark clouds made the daytime suddenly become night.

Greg held onto the wooden stake in his left hand and gently laid the hammer down on the coffin between his legs. With his trembling right hand, he reached for the latch to unlock the coffin. Sweat began to pour down his face and his heart raced. With one swift move, he quickly opened the dark brown coffin.

"She's not in here!" he yelled with a hint of relief in his voice.

Earl and Cory were now looking down into the grave while the wind continued to howl ferociously around them.

Earl stared at the dark, gray sky.

"Earl, what's wrong? What happened to the sun?" Greg asked.

"Let's get out of here," said Earl.

The three men raced back through the old graveyard as the wind swirled dust and debris at them. At one point, a large tree limb barely missed Earl's head. It appeared as if some unseen force had hurled the limb directly at the seventy-three-year-old man. Greg lowered his head against the wind. Even though the truck was only fifty yards from Loretta's grave, it seemed to him like it was five miles.

Finally, all three men made it back to the truck. Greg jumped in the driver's side and quickly started the engine. He threw the truck into reverse and stomped on the gas pedal, causing the tires to spin madly out of control. He turned and navigated the truck backwards through the black gate and onto the road. A mile down the road, the bright autumn sunshine suddenly blinded their eyes.

"That's weird. Where did all this sunshine come from?" Cory asked.

"That's not a weather anomaly," said Earl.

"What are you talking about Earl?" Greg asked, still breathing heavily.

"I've been thinkin' about those articles I found on the Internet. I'm beginning to believe that we're in a deep spiritual battle for our town," Earl replied, looking over his glasses at Greg. He continued. "Have you ever wondered why most folks in Plainridge don't go to church?"

"I never really gave it much thought growing up, but I began to notice, when I moved back last year, that the town was spiritually dead. I guess as a kid, I never picked up on it," Greg replied.

"Well, I've noticed it my whole life. Heck, we've got two bars, but only one church," Earl stated, shifting around in the passenger seat. Greg could tell that the old man was starting to get worked up. "For heaven's sake, we live in the Bible belt. Most towns in the South aren't like this."

"I never grew up going to church and neither did my folks," Cory said. "If it hadn't been for Greg, I would've never asked Jesus to save me, and I would've died in the Lynch house."

"Greg, have you ever talked to Reverend Wilson about the spiritual state of the town?" Earl asked.

"Yeah, I causally broached the subject with him a few weeks after I moved back, but he acted like he had no idea what I was talking about. Actually, I never see him except on Sundays. He's always in his parish. I don't know what he does."

"Well, Wilson's been the minister here since 1960, so that doesn't surprise me," Earl responded.

"Greg, I saw him leaving his parish one day last week. I'd come by looking for you. He was acting all weird and all," Cory said.

"What do you mean weird?"

"He was leaving his parish and locking the dead bolt on the door. He kept grabbing the doorknob and trying to turn it, like he was making sure it was locked up. I kinda startled him when I walked up behind him."

By this time, they were coming back into town. Greg slowed down as they cruised down Taylor Street. Other than Doyle's Auto Repair and Joe's Pub & Grill, most stores on Taylor had been closed for years. Boarded up windows and vacant brick buildings reflected the economic state of the town.

"What should we do next?" Greg asked.

"I think we need to talk to someone who can tell us more about the history of our town. What's the root of this evil that keeps our town suppressed spiritually?" Earl stated.

"You mean, there's someone who knows more than you?" Cory asked.

"There's a lot of folks who know more than me, but few who'll talk to us. However, there is one."

"Who's that?" Greg asked.

"The widow Crenshaw."

Greg's head quickly turned to Earl. "You wanna go see that old witch?" Greg asked with a look of disbelief. Even though he'd never been to the Crenshaw place, Greg was well aware of the rumors of what happens to people who visit Old Lady Crenshaw.

For generations, the Crenshaw house had been widely regarded as being haunted. The prevailing rumor, most folks considered a fact, was that Old Lady Crenshaw was a witch, which people explained was the reason she continued to live well into her nineties. Like many similar places in the South, it was an old, mysterious place surrounded by local folklore and legend. It was a place where teenagers dared one another to visit after dark—even though most parents forbade it—and embellished stories that had been passed down from one generation to the next, stories that kept smaller kids up most of the night.

Cory let out a long, deep sigh from the back. "When I was kid, we were told that Old Lady Crenshaw was a witch and her house was haunted." Cory used both hands to pull himself forward, closer to Earl. For some reason, that topic seemed to hit a nerve with him. "The story was if she saw you, she would eventually come for you when the moon was full. Do we really have to go there?"

"I had a dream the other night that I went to see her. I think she might have some information that could be the key that unlocks all this," Earl replied.

"When do you want to go see her?" Greg asked.

"Let's head out there later this afternoon, but let's stop and grab a bite at my house first."

Even though he tried to downplay the rumors surrounding Old Lady Crenshaw and the Crenshaw home, Earl secretly wondered if this was a mistake.

29 October 1858

I received the most interesting invitation today. A courier, whom I have never seen before, delivered it to my house late this afternoon. It was addressed to me and only my name appeared on the front of the envelope. Inside was a note from Hester Lynch, inviting me to attend a meeting at the Lynch Plantation on the 31st of October at midnight. According to the note, the purpose of the meeting is to discuss a solution to our town's terrible drought.

I am fully aware of the rumors regarding Mr. Lynch and his plantation, but I dare not attend for fear of what might happen to me.

From the diary of Dorothy Lee
October 29, 1858

SEVEN

The Crenshaw farm was located several miles off County Road 10. It was a remote place that people didn't simply stumble upon. One had to know how to get there. Levi Crenshaw was one of the town's original founders. An immigrant from Northern Wales, Levi brought his family over to the United States in 1824 as famine swept through Western Europe. Not long after arriving, Levi was able to acquire several acres south of town and immediately began farming cotton, corn, and beans.

A year later, Crenshaw formed a friendship with a pig farmer named Charles Brown and together they decided to form the town of Crossville. The town charter was signed in early 1825—merely fifty years after America had won its independence from England and only thirty years before the country would find itself fighting its own Civil War.

Levi and Charles were both devout in their Christian faith and shared the belief that their friendship had been a divine appointment to form a town in the new world. It was well known that both Levi Crenshaw and Charles Brown were the only two men in the surrounding area who chose not to own African Americans as slaves, even though there were rare occasions when they purchased slaves in order to keep families together, only to set them free later. Both men abhorred the idea of slavery and were known for their honest business dealings and for caring for their workers. During the Civil War, it was suspected that both Crenshaw and Brown worked with the Underground Railroad to help many slaves escape to the North.

Cotton was king in the South in the 1840s and 1850s, and everyone thrived with the economic boom. In the town of Crossville, cotton looked like fallen snowflakes in the fields and could been seen as far as the eye could see. Hester Lynch, born in the winter of 1799 to a poor Irish farmer, started his plantation not far from the Crenshaw farm in 1830. By the late 1840s, Lynch had become the wealthiest man in town, mainly by using slave labor. A very greedy and arrogant man, Lynch was considered the most powerful man in town and was notorious for his shrewd business dealings and cruelty toward his slaves. His sinister black carriage was frequently seen strolling down Main Street, usually near the bank. Always draped in a black cloak and tall, black hat, Lynch's tall, slender frame and unorthodox appearance struck fear in the citizens of Crossville. There were rumors around town that he practiced black magic and was in league with the devil, which people explained was the reason for his strange powers of persuasion. Once a month, Lynch would make a trip to Montgomery to purchase new slaves at the weekly slave auction. Due to the harsh working conditions and lack of care, many slaves died while working at the Lynch plantation.

Life was good in Crossville and everyone prospered, until the great drought in the summer of 1857 hit the Deep South. For three straight years, very little rain combined with relentless heat caused cotton and other crops to die. The once fertile cotton fields were turned into dust bowls. Many farm animals died as the town desperately tried to survive. However, Levi Crenshaw and Charles Brown seemed to miraculously prosper during this difficult time.

***

It was dusk when Earl's truck rumbled down County Road 10 toward the Crenshaw farm. Earl had only been to the Crenshaw place once when he was a boy. His daddy had some business dealings with Jacob Crenshaw—Levi's grandson—and took Earl along with him. As Earl steered his truck down the desolate road, he vividly recalled the memory of meeting Jacob Crenshaw and standing beneath the twenty-foot-tall wooden cross that stood directly in front of their house.

Earl took his foot off the accelerator and slowly turned off County Road 10 and onto a hidden, narrow, one-lane dirt road that would take them to the Crenshaw house. Greg looked at the vast acres of withered cornstalks as the tires on Earl's truck threw dirt and dust up in the cool, dry air. "What if she's not there?" Cory asked.

"Don't worry; she's always there," Earl replied.

They quickly approached the old house and, with the sun fading in the distance, the three men could clearly see the large, ominous cross casting its long shadow across the house. The Crenshaw house looked more like a white sharecropper's house than the large plantation house that Greg had imagined. A tin roof, rotten wooden planks, and dangling window shutters reflected the age of the home, but the thing that grabbed Greg's attention were the numerous crosses that appeared on each window of the house.

"What's up with all the crosses?" Greg asked.

"I told y'all that she knows all about the history of our town," Earl responded, parking his truck next to the gigantic cross.

Greg and Cory got out of the truck with apprehension, slowly taking in the place. The old, rundown house was surrounded by acres and acres of brown cornstalks, or what used to be cornstalks now that summer had ended. On the front porch, an old lady was gently rocking in a wooden chair and shucking green beans into a metallic bowl while singing an old hymn. Her stringy, white hair covered a portion of her face and her plain, black dress looked ragged, just like her. Greg could tell that her old, wrinkled face had seen plenty of hot Alabama summers. She had a long, protruding nose and pointed chin, which were only accentuated by her wide, piercing eyes. Her hands and long, bony fingers looked like brown leather. She continued to shuck green beans, seemingly unaware of their presence. She softly sang a hymn while staring out into the cornfields with her cold, blue eyes, which gave her the appearance of being blind.

**The Crenshaw witch as depicted by Edgar Hamilton,
Plainridge Public Library**

"'Tis so sweet to trust in Jesus, just to take Him at
His Word . . ."

"Hello there," Earl hollered, wading through the
knee-high grass, making his way from the truck to the steps
of the porch.

"Earl Smith, I knew you were comin'," the widow
replied, in a crackling voice with a thick Southern drawl. She
continued to stare into the fields over the three men who

had not yet made their way onto the porch. "I had a dream the other night that you'd be comin' to see me. What is it that you desire, Earl Smith?"

Her voice gave Greg chills up his spine. He felt like he had entered into a time warp and was back in the 1800s. *What did she mean, she knew we were coming?*

"I've brought some friends with me," Earl replied.

"I know what y'all's seeking," replied the widow. "It's not of this world."

Cory hoped they wouldn't get any closer. The sound of her voice gave him the creeps. The stories he had heard as a kid about the Crenshaw place being haunted all came back at once. He recalled a story that an older kid had once told him one day after school about the widow being a witch and coming into town when the moon was full to take kids back to her house, where she would eat them. Cory remembered the older boy telling him that when you heard a tap on your window and the moon was full, then that meant the Crenshaw witch had come for you. All his childhood fears seemed to resurface at once. He stayed a couple of feet behind Greg, close to the truck, next to the large cross. Earl took a few more steps toward the wooden steps that led to the front porch, but appeared reluctant to walk up them.

"Papa told me when I was a little girl that Hester Lynch was an evil man and to stay away from the Lynch house. You see, it all started back with the great drought in the late 1850s, before the War of Northern Aggression. Papa said that Hester, like most folks in town, went broke during that time. There wasn't any water, the crops burnt up, and the farm animals died. He lost everything, but the Lynch house. Hester hated my great-granddaddy, Levi.

"Widow, why did your papa tell you to stay away from the Lynch house?" An eerie laugh proceeded out the widow Crenshaw's mouth, revealing her bare gums. "You know why, Earl Smith. You saw that abomination last year. That's why he built this here cross."

"But how did Hester become a vampire?" Earl asked.

"During the great drought, folks became desperate and instead of turning to the Lord, they turned away from God. Hester Lynch called a secret meeting at his house and all the town leaders, except for Levi Crenshaw and Charles Brown were invited. The meeting was held at midnight on October 31, and it was there that Hester persuaded them that their God had forsaken them. He told them the only way for their wealth to be restored was to renounce their faith in God. That night, a secret covenant was made and a new town charter was signed in blood.

"Reverend Silas protested and stormed out of the meeting. The next morning he was found hung under the large oak tree beside the church. His body hung there for several days."

"What happened next?" Earl asked, glancing up at the moon and stars shining brightly in the night sky. The sun had finally set beneath the horizon and nighttime had suddenly enveloped the sky like a black curtain. The widow Crenshaw did not immediately answer, but rocked back and forth in her chair, continuing to stare into the open fields as if she were in some sort of trance.

Finally, she spoke. "The rain finally came, but at a terrible price!" she exclaimed. "Folks started gettin' sick for no reason. Their crops got eaten by insects and their animals got diseases and died. Right before the war, my great-granddaddy, Levi, got sick and died. Charles Brown decided to sell his farm and move away from this evil place."

"But what about Hester Lynch?" Earl asked, wishing she would get on with the story. He wasn't comfortable being out there now that it was nighttime. The only visible light came from a kerosene lantern that sat on a table next to the front window. The full moon hung high in the night sky creating a chilling image of the old woman as she continued to rock back and forth, apparently in deep thought. Greg had moved back to the truck next to Cory. Both appeared ready to jump into the truck at any moment.

The temperature was dropping fast, and the cold north wind began to gain strength. Earl suddenly jumped and quickly looked over his left shoulder; a sudden gust of wind blew through, rattling the cornstalks. It sounded like something was walking through the cornstalks, coming up behind him. At last, she spoke; he could see her breath through the crisp, thin air. "That's when the evil one showed up. Years later, during the War of Northern Aggression, Hester wandered out, early one morning before dawn, to look after his cattle. He was approached by a wounded Confederate soldier or what he thought was a wounded soldier . . ." There was a brief pause as the widow turned and for the first time locked eyes with Earl. Earl immediately took a step back toward his truck. Her piercing eyes looked right through him, and he did his best not to make eye contact.

"Hester went over to attend to the young soldier, who had fallen to the ground. He was surprised when the soldier grabbed him and buried his fangs into his neck."

"What happened to that soldier?" Earl yelled, with his hand next to his mouth.

"I reckon Hester killed him or the sun burnt him up. Not long afterwards, my granddaddy, Joshua, said that he saw Hester wandering up on our farm late one evening with an evil look on his face. He was dirty, like he'd crawled out of the earth. Joshua went outside to meet him, but when Hester saw the cross around his neck, he hissed, covered his face, and ran into the woods. That's when Granddaddy put a cross on our front door. Later on, he built this here cross and told me never to go near the Lynch house."

"So, it was Hester who wandered into town in the spring of 1864 and took some woman and children?" Earl asked.

"Yes!" the widow responded emphatically, leaning forward in her rocking chair. "He needed blood. It's part of the curse."

Stunned by this new information, Earl decided it was time to leave. "I guess we'd better head on back to town. Thank you for your help, Widow."

"Be careful, Earl Smith. The enemy knows what y'all are up to," the old woman replied.

Earl turned and began walking swiftly back to his truck.

"He desires to set the town free and to make it new!" the widow hollered from her chair.

Earl shouted back at the old woman, with one foot inside the truck and his hand resting on the truck's open window. "How do we set the town free? Kill Loretta?"

The old woman started that sinister laugh again, looking directly at the three men. In her thick, Southern accent she replied, "She's already dead." There was another brief pause. Cory had already crawled into the backseat of the truck. Greg stood on the passenger side with the door open. He felt comforted knowing that he could jump into the truck and lock the door if he had to. Then the old woman stood up from her chair and took a few steps forward. *I hope she's not coming over here,* Earl thought.

She lifted her long, bony finger, pointed toward the woods behind them, and said, "The ground's cursed. The town's cursed." That was enough. Earl and Greg both jumped into the truck and slammed their doors shut. Greg immediately reached over and locked his door. Earl quickly cranked the truck, put it in reverse, and rapidly backed up. Greg noticed the goose bumps that seemed to stand an inch high on Earl's arms.

Greg continued to study the old woman from his passenger mirror, watching her slowly go back into her broken down house. He was jolted in his seat when Earl hit a large pothole, which had been concealed by the darkness. He sped down the dirt road to County Road 10.

With his long, skinny fingers, Deputy Sims frantically pounded Mayor Watson's home phone number into his cell phone. He was taking long, deep breaths, trying to compose himself. After several rings, he finally heard the mayor's voice on the other end. "Hello?"

"Mayor Watson, it's me, Deputy Sims."

"Hello, Deputy, how can I help you?"

"I found the sheriff; actually, I'm at his house right now. I came up here looking for him, since we never heard from him today." There was a short pause as the deputy gathered himself. "Mayor, he's dead, and it looks like he's been dead for several hours."

"Any idea, what happened?"

"No, sir, but half his throat's missing."

Those words jarred Ed Watson to his core. His insides twisted. "Say that again, Deputy."

"Mayor, it looks like he was thrown through the window of his house and that someone took a knife or some weapon and ripped his throat out. What should we do?"

In a calm, soothing voice the mayor replied, "Deputy, I want you to listen very closely to what I'm about to tell you."

"Yes sir."

"I want you to put his body in the back of your patrol car and clean up any blood and evidence in the area. Do you understand?"

"Yes sir."

"I'll meet you in forty-five minutes at the funeral home, and we'll take it from there."

"Mayor Watson?"

"Yes?"

"Do you think it was her?"

"Just do as I say and everything will be okay, all right?"

"Yes sir, 10–4."

Mayor Watson hung up the phone, turned ghostly pale, and collapsed into his chair in deep thought.

"Honey, who called?"

Ed Watson did not immediately answer his wife, but continued in deep thought, with his hands interlaced underneath his chin.

"Honey?" His wife had made her way into the den. "Who was that on the phone?"

"Nothing important, dear. Hey, uh, do we still have a cross somewhere in the house?"

EIGHT

Happy hour was in full swing at Joe's Pub & Grill. It was 6:30 p.m. and most of the employees from Crown Manufacturing were already on their second round of drinks. George Sikes sat alone at the end of the bar, his head buried in his hands, mumbling to himself. Joe Skinner, the owner, was feverishly wiping down the bar counter, while making sure everyone's drink was full. The large, flat-screen television above the bar was tuned to ESPN, and sounds of pinball machines buzzed and clicked in the background.

"Why . . . Why . . . ," George muttered underneath his breath. He'd barely touched his drink, and appeared consumed with grief.

"Hey George, you doin' okay down there?" Joe hollered from behind the bar. "You need another drink?"

There was no answer, but folks had learned to stay away from George Sikes ever since he began telling everyone he'd seen Loretta and that she'd come back to him. The word around town was that he'd lost his mind, even though some residents secretly suspected the worst.

"NO!" came a sudden, but emphatic outburst as George slammed his fist down on the counter, causing his drink to spill over the sides of his glass. With the exception of the television and pinball machines, silence filled the air. Several of the pub's best patrons began putting on their jackets and heading for the door. That was the last thing that Joe Skinner wanted to see during his most important business hour.

Joe slowly made his way over to George, leaned over the counter, and whispered into his ear, "Hey George, what's wrong? I know it's been a tough year for ya, but I can't have you scaring my customers away. You understand, don't ya?"

"Why, Loretta . . . why?" George snorted, looking away from Skinner as if he didn't even hear him at all.

"What happened, George? Did you see Loretta again?" he asked, trying to somehow humor his friend.

George Sikes finally looked up and made eye contact with him. "It was last night, I . . . uh, I remember waking up and seeing her looking at me through our bedroom window. I got up and went to the window."

"Yeah, that's good ain't it, George? I know how much you miss her."

"NO!" George responded, slamming his fist on the dark, wooden counter.

"What do you mean, no?" Joe replied, taking a step back.

"It was my Loretta aight, but she looked different. I– I got the feeling she wanted to hurt me."

"Well, that was creepy," Greg muttered, scanning both sides of the road, not wanting to be surprised by Loretta again.

"Yeah, after that, I'm not so sure the stories I heard as a kid aren't true," Cory said.

Earl was strangely silent all the way back into town. Greg thought he looked a little shaken after the encounter with the widow, but maybe he was just as nervous about Loretta darting out in front of them as she had done the previous evening. Finally, Greg looked over to Earl and asked him, "So, what'd you think?"

"'Bout what?" Earl responded, being somewhat coy.

"About, what the widow said," Greg replied with a puzzled look. He could tell Earl was shutting down on him. He knew more than he was letting on. Something the widow said really bothered him, *but what was it?*

Greg was about to ask him another question when his cell phone rang. It was Rachel. "Hey honey."

"Greg, where are you?"

Something was wrong. He could sense it. "I'm with Earl and Cory, what's wrong, honey?"

"It all started after you left last night. I couldn't sleep. Every time the house creaked, I jumped. I kept hearing noises outside my window. I don't know, maybe I was just imaging it."

"I'll be there in just a few minutes, okay?" Greg replied.

"Greg please hurry, something else happened at school today, and it really freaked me out. I've been trying to reach you all afternoon."

At 7:00 p.m., Mayor Watson turned into the parking lot of Akin's Funeral Home. The aging funeral parlor was owned by Jim Akin, who also served as the town's coroner. The short, bald, heavyset, sixty-eight-year-old Akin was standing at the front door waiting on his old friend to make his way inside. His beady eyes scanned the parking lot, and his bearded face had a look of deep concern. He had been caught off guard when Ed Watson phoned him a little less than an hour ago, informing him of the sheriff's demise.

He briefly reflected back to this time last year when John Hayes had brought Loretta Sikes into the funeral home. He remembered seeing the two small puncture wounds on the upper part of her left shoulder, which at the time caused him great concern, along with her a small, faint heartbeat. During the examination, John informed him of what had just occurred at the Lynch house, and they both decided to call Mayor Watson before taking the next step.

In secret, the three men agreed to bury Loretta Sikes in the back of Asbury Cemetery that night. John Hayes arrogantly assured them that this was the best option and that nothing could escape five feet of earth, vampire, or human. Together, they would destroy the town's secret and no one would ever know, even if this meant the possibility of murder. Plainridge's dark past would be forgotten forever. No need to ask for forgiveness. No need to repent for past sins. No need for God. Just move on with pursuing the pleasures of life.

Akin swiftly opened the door for the mayor, who pressed his hands into his jacket pockets and walked slightly bent over, bracing himself against the stiff, autumn wind. It had turned unusually cold for this time of year. The strong north wind served as a reminder that the cold darkness of winter was just around the corner.

"Where's Deputy Sims?" Jim Akin remarked, while holding the door open for the mayor to make his way inside the funeral home.

The funeral home was dark on the inside. The only light came from a dimly lit old brass light fixture in the foyer where the two men were standing. "He should be here any minute," the mayor responded. "I told 'im to clean up any evidence at John's house. I'll call the hardware store tomorrow and order a new window. I'll put it in myself."

"That'll work," Akin replied. "I'll just tell folks that it was an apparent heart attack and that he died sittin' in his favorite chair."

"What about his throat? Sims said it looked pretty bad."

"Don't worry about that. I'll fix it and cover it up with a nice shirt and tie," Akin confidently responded. "Any news on those missing teenagers?"

"Nope. Last thing John told me was it didn't look promising. He mentioned the idea of a bear attack. I thought he could sell it, but he needed to wrap it up before any outsiders showed up."

Akin nodded in agreement.

"So, uh . . . do you think it was her?" Watson asked.

Akin responded with an icy stare.

At that time, they both turned around as the car lights from Deputy Sims' patrol car flashed across the glass door.

"'Bout time," Akin remarked, walking past the mayor out the front door.

"Where's the body?" Akin asked in a sharp, condescending tone, just as the deputy was slamming his car door shut.

"He's in the back. I'll tell ya, he's a lot lighter than I thought he'd be. I'd thought I was gonna have a dickens of a time gettin' him in my patrol car all by myself and all," the deputy replied.

"Hurry up; I don't want anybody to see us dragging him in here."

Deputy Sims ran quickly around to the passenger side of the patrol car, opened the back door, and grabbed the sheriff by his boots and began dragging him out of the car. Watson, hands still buried in his pockets, stood at the back of the car, blocking the view from anyone who might be watching them. Jim Akin grabbed hold of the sheriff's upper torso and they quickly carried him inside the funeral home.

The two men carried the sheriff's lifeless body down the dark, narrow hallway toward the very back where the bodies were prepared for funeral. They headed toward the preparation room where the toxic smell of embalming fluid and other chemicals became overwhelming. They laid the body on a cold, metal examining table. Jim Akin put on his white lab coat and began searching for all his tools to begin the autopsy.

"Told ya he wadn't that heavy," the skinny deputy said, leaning up against the wall trying to regain his breath.

"Hmmm . . . interesting, very interesting . . . ," mumbled Akin as he closely examined the throat and neck area. By now, Mayor Watson had locked the front door and made his way down the hall and into the cold room.

"What is it?" Ed Watson asked, trying to gauge the coroner's face.

"Looks like all the main arteries have been vacated."

"What does that mean? In simple terms, please," replied Watson, raising one eyebrow.

Akin looked up at Ed Watson. In a serious but matter-of-fact manner, he said, "It means that most of the blood in his body is gone."

***

Greg raced from his jeep down the cracked, uneven sidewalk and swiftly up the steps to Rachel's front porch. He had heard the fear in her voice and just wanted to get to her, to hold her. Even though she only lived a short distance from Earl's house, it seemed to take forever to get there. He pounded on her front door with his fist, causing the wooden cross to jiggle up and down.

"RACH? IT'S ME, GREG!" he yelled through the door.

A moment later, he heard the deadbolt unlock. She swiftly opened the door and wrapped her arms around his waist. She was still shaking. He could tell by the black smudges on her face that she'd been crying. He held her tight, feeling a sense of relief. *I got you now.*

She loved being held in his strong arms. All her fears seemed to go away, and now they both felt like they could stay this way forever. After several minutes, Greg unlocked his hands from around her waist and gently led her over to the couch.

"Rachel, what happened today? I've never seen you this upset."

"Greg, you know how I told you I couldn't sleep last night?"

"Uh huh."

"Well, when I got to school this morning, it got worse. I don't know, maybe I'm losing my mind," she said, covering both hands over her face.

"What are you talking about, Rach? What happened at school?"

"I was walking down the hall in the elementary school when I saw a picture taped on a wall outside a third-grade classroom. You know the kind that kids draw about their family. Well, one of the pictures caught my attention. The face on the picture was a woman with long, dark hair, but the face was so evil. I couldn't quit staring at it. I thought about your story the other night about seeing Loretta on County Road 10, so I took the picture off the wall and went into the classroom. I asked the teacher who drew the picture, and she pointed to a little girl in the corner. I went over and asked the little girl who this was supposed to be." There was a brief pause. Rachel swallowed hard and tried to compose herself. Then she turned and looked into Greg's eyes and said, "The little girl told me that it was the lady who comes to her window every night and stares at her in bed."

"Rach, what did you do with the picture?"

"I brought it home; I wanted you to see it." Rachel got up and went over to her backpack. She pulled out the picture and handed it to Greg. All the color left his face as he studied the drawing.

"Greg, I really think this is a spiritual thing. Please, let's just pack up and leave this town. We can leave tomorrow, go somewhere where it's warm and sunny. We can get married and just forget about this place."

Greg reached over and put both arms around his fiancée, and pulled her close to him. He knew what she was feeling, and he knew she was right. This was spiritual. He had witnessed the same evil first hand last year at the Lynch house. Part of him wanted to leave, but he knew he couldn't abandon his friends, not now. Loretta was obviously moving around town. She needed blood. *We have to find her and end this.*

NINE

That night, Earl tossed and turned in his bed. He couldn't get the widow Crenshaw out of his mind. Each time he closed his eyes, he could still see her sitting on her front porch, her steel blue eyes staring right through him. His thoughts raced back and forth on what she had told them. The small, two-bedroom house he'd lived in his entire adult life was uncomfortably quiet. He could hear the squeaks of the old house settling underneath him while the north wind howled outside his bedroom window. *Were any of my ancestors involved in that meeting?* He wrestled with that question.

Part of him wished that the old woman had never mentioned the secret meeting and new town charter. In all his years of studying the town's history, he had never heard this story. He wondered if his father, grandfather, or great-grandfather knew about the true dark history of Crossville. Furthermore, were they involved? He had to find out, but how? He sat up on the edge of his bed and began rubbing his wrinkled face. Then it occurred to him. *John Hayes knew more about this town than he ever let on. I know he has Dorothy Lee's diary. I bet there's more information at his house. I should go there before the mayor and deputy take all his personal belongings, if they haven't already. Tomorrow will be too late for sure. I don't want to go tonight. What if she's there?*

The old man instinctively rose from his bed and began pacing back and forth across the cold, hardwood floor. He glanced over at the clock on his nightstand—1:00 a.m. it read in large, bright red digits. *What should I do? This may be my only chance to ever know the truth.* He immediately started getting dressed. His desire to know the truth was winning the battle over his fear. He slid his familiar brown cowboy boots on and headed for the front door. *I can be there by 1:30. It won't take that long to find what I'm looking for.* As he grabbed his jacket off the coat rack, he noticed, out of the corner of his eye, a silver crucifix lying on the kitchen table. He had planned on putting it on his front door earlier that day. Earl paused for a moment, staring at the bright cross. He then walked over, put it in his jacket pocket, turned and headed out the door into the night.

***

The curtains were drawn tight against the bedroom window. George Sikes shivered under the covers in fear, trying to survive another long night. *Maybe she won't come tonight,* he thought as he listened for the slightest movement outside his window. The windy evening made it that much harder to detect any unusual sound. It had been weeks since he had a good night's rest. Then a bump up against the side of the house caused him to jerk in bed. *It's okay, George; it was just a branch, that's all. Just a few more hours and it'll be dawn.*

Those were his last conscious thoughts before drifting into a deep dream. He found himself back in elementary school trying hard to pay attention. He'd never been a good student and once again found himself in trouble. His best friend, Billy Brasher, had just passed him a note and the teacher, Mrs. Hoskins, had turned around just in time to see it. His stomach sank when he saw her making her way toward his desk. Everyone immediately focused their eyes on their own paper and dared not look up. Now looming above him, her once sweet smile had morphed into a sinister grin that made George's blood run cold. The slow tilt of her head was in sync with the widening of her wicked grin. Sharp, white fangs suddenly appeared behind an evil smile, and her smooth skin became wrinkled and gaunt. She seemed to revel in the fear on George's face. "AHHHHH!" he screamed, jumping straight up in bed. He leaned back against his pillow and let out a loud sigh. "It was just a dream, George, that's all. I wish I could get some sleep," he mumbled while rolling over on his left side. Then he heard it, the strangely familiar tapping, followed by prolonged scraping against the bedroom window. It was always at the same time.

Oh no! Not again, please not again. The tapping continued. *Tap . . . Tap . . . Tap . . . Scr-e-e-ch . . .* He covered his ears and pulled the covers over his head. *Maybe she'll go away.* He was startled by the sound of glass shattering. He seemed to hear all the small fragments hitting the floor at the same time. He lay there motionless, trying hard not to move, and then the sweetest voice came from outside the window.

"George, darling, please let me in. I'm so cold."

He missed hearing her tender, sweet voice. He began to weep. *Is this just another bad dream?*

Then he heard her voice again. "George, please, I want to come in. I'm cold and I miss you."

Consumed with grief, George Sikes found himself crawling out of bed and making his way over to the small, paint-chipped bedroom window. He stood completely still facing the shattered window and white curtain. The room was cold; he could see his breath each time he exhaled. His hand trembled reaching for the lock. Startled, he let out a horrific scream when Loretta pulled back the curtain.

***

The heater in his truck was on full blast as he blazed down County Road 10 toward John's Hayes' house. Earl had placed the silver crucifix and his pistol next to him in the truck, just in case something happened along the way. He wasn't sure why he'd gotten his pistol out the glove compartment. He knew deep down it wouldn't help, but just the thought of having it close gave him some comfort. He still struggled with the thought that one of his ancestors could have been part of that secret meeting on that fateful night at the Lynch house. His deep desire to know the truth compelled him to keep going.

Finally, he pulled off County Road 10 and onto the dark, one-lane driveway that led to the former sheriff's house. A beautiful golden harvest moon shined brightly behind the dark house. Two large trees on both sides of the house were being bent back and forth from the strong, hard north wind. He had not stopped to think about the sheriff's body. *Is it still there? I wonder if Mayor Watson and Deputy Sims have been out here yet.*

Loretta Sikes

He pulled close to the front steps and placed the truck in park. The old man sat there momentarily, studying the house, debating if he'd made the right decision by coming out here. Finally, he reached over and grabbed his pistol and crucifix along with a flashlight from the glove compartment. Earl stepped outside his truck and immediately flinched against the cold, autumn wind. He zipped up his tan jacket and made his way up the steps and onto the front porch. He decided to check the front door first. To his surprise, it was unlocked. The door made a loud creaking sound when he opened it. He clicked his flashlight on and slowly walked into the old house. He stood next to the door and shined the light around the dark room. *Okay, where's the light switch.* He turned and shined his flashlight up against the wood panel wall next to the door, searching for the switch. *Found it. Shoot!* He flipped on all the switches, but no power. *Power's out. Must've been the wind that got the power lines.*

What do I do now? Fear was beginning to win. The old man took a couple steps forward and almost tripped over a kitchen chair. The darkness was thick and suffocating. He tried hard to adjust his eyes to the darkness. He was near the shattered window now and decided to take a quick peek to see if the sheriff's body was still lying on the side porch. Cautiously, he moved forward and glanced outside the window. Not only was the body gone, but he could tell that someone had cleaned up all the blood and glass. *They've been here. I wonder if they took the time to go through his stuff. Now's my only chance.*

Earl began thinking hard. *Where would John keep all his personal possessions?* He stood perfectly still and shined the flashlight around the den, past the sheriff's favorite chair. *Not down here. He wouldn't chance that. There's not a basement. It has to be upstairs.* Taking his time, the old man made his way through the cluttered den and crept around the corner to the stairs that led to the second floor of the house. He was greeted instantly by a thick spiderweb as he began to make his way up the dark, wooden steps. The wood creaked loudly with each step he took. Once he had made it all the way to the top, he saw three closed doors—one in the middle and one on each side facing each other. *I wonder which one was his bedroom. Let's start with the middle door.*

Reaching with his left hand, while holding the flashlight with his right, Earl slowly twisted the knob that opened John Hayes' bedroom door. He was surprised to see spiderwebs covering the entire room. He could tell no one had been up here in quite a long time. The bright moon shined through the bedroom window, providing him additional lighting, while creating an eerie atmosphere. Just above the fully made, undisturbed bed was an enormous, intricately woven spiderweb that crisscrossed the large bed like a canopy.

Scanning the room with his flashlight, he noticed a large, black iron safe in the right-hand corner. "Bingo!" he said to himself, breaking through spiderwebs and making his way over to the safe. He squatted down and began studying the old, dusty safe. The safe contained a handle on the left side and an old combination lock on the front. He wiped an inch of dust off the lock and carefully examined it with his flashlight. *Where's his secret combination? I wonder if he kept it in the house?* Instinctively, Earl grabbed the handle on the side and pulled. Not expecting anything to happen, he was stunned and happy when the iron door cracked open.

"Whoohoo!" yelled the old man in jubilee. He couldn't believe his good fortune. He pulled the heavy door open and shined his flashlight inside. The inside of the safe contained a top and bottom shelf. On the top shelf rested a small leather-bound book. He'd seen that book before. He grabbed it and immediately recognized it was Dorothy Lee's diary.

It was the same book the sheriff had showed him last October when he revealed to Earl that he was a descendant of Dorothy Lee. Earl was beyond tickled. He had long desired to read this diary ever since he held it in his hands last October. Next, he began to rummage through the bottom shelf. He pulled out several old documents that were layered in dust.

How did John obtain all these documents? he wondered. One particular document caught his attention. It was approximately a foot long and rolled up. It appeared to be very old. Earl reached for the brown document and gently pulled it out of the safe. He could tell it had been written on parchment paper and had to be well over one hundred years old. He slowly and gently unrolled the document across the dusty floor. He reached over and grabbed his flashlight, which was lying next to him. With his back toward the door, he began reading the ancient scroll. It was the town charter. He had found it. The widow Crenshaw was right. Earl read the document in silence; he couldn't believe what he was reading. The ink had faded over time, but he could still make out several words. He was both horrified and disgusted at the same time.

31 OCTOBER 1858

WHEREAS, WE THE CITIZENS OF CROSSVILLE, ON THIS THIRTY-FIRST NIGHT OF OCTOBER, EIGHTEEN HUNRDRED AND FIFTY EIGHT, BY AN ACT OF OUR FREE WILL, CALL UPON LUCIFER, THE PRINCE OF DARKNESS, TO BRING US RAIN AND TO RESTORE OUR WEALTH. WHEREAS, WE THE CITIZENS OF CROSSVILLE, THEREFORE AND UNTO RENOUNCE GOD THE FATHER, GOD THE SON, AND GOD THE HOLY SPIRIT. BY AN ACT OF OUR FREE WILL, WE HENCEFORTH PROCLAIM THAT WE ALONE ARE MASTERS OF OUR OWN DESTINY AND OFFER THEE OUR TOWNSHIP IN RETURN FOR RAIN, CROPS, AND WEALTH.

Earl felt vomit rising up in his throat. He swallowed hard, studying the signatures at the bottom of the page. Many of the names were faded. He held the flashlight close to the document and read the names out loud. "Joseph A. Crawford, James E. Earl, Henry Swords, Dorothy Lee, William Buckner, George Fletcher, Hester R. Lynch."

After studying the signatures for several moments, he felt relieved that none of the names on the list were from his ancestry. *Were these the only people who knew?* he pondered. Then a sound from downstairs suddenly zapped back his attention. *What was that? Could just be the wind,* the old man told himself, rapidly collecting all the documents from the safe. It was time to go; there would be plenty of time to read through all the documents at his house.

With the flashlight in his right hand and the documents cradled in both arms, Earl swiftly turned toward the door to leave. "AHHHH!" he screamed and fell backwards against the hardwood floor, sending a cloud of dust into the air. The old documents flew in every direction. Earl sat on the floor covered in spiderwebs staring at Loretta Sikes. Her ghostly face was hideous. He could see the splattered, dried blood on her chin. From deep within her came a low growl, followed by an eerie laugh that chilled his blood.

Her demonic face was contorted and full of rage and hate. Earl pressed the palm of his hands against the dusty, wooden floor as he began frantically trying to back up. After a couple of pushes, his head hit the bedroom wall. He was trapped. She just stood there, a few feet in front of him, staring at him, like a beast that had cornered its prey. But for some reason, she seemed to be keeping her distance. *Why doesn't she attack me?* Earl wondered.

He found himself both intrigued and horrified at the same time. He noticed that her dress was ragged and dirty, like she had just crawled out of the ground. Light from the moon beamed into the bedroom and onto Loretta, creating a frightening image. It was at that moment that Earl realized, *This isn't Loretta; it's evil personified.* He then suddenly remembered the cross in his jacket pocket. He reached into his right pocket, grabbed the silver cross tightly, and held it up to the vampire. "I command you in the name of Jesus of Nazareth, to leave me alone. You have no power over me!" he yelled, standing to his feet. Earl took one step forward, continuing to hold the crucifix. "I am under the blood of Jesus, the Son of the highest God. Leave this place now in Jesus' name."

The vampire let out a loud, high-pitch, agonizing scream that resonated throughout the empty house. Earl felt the hair on the back of neck stand straight up. She then turned, ran, and jumped through the bedroom window, crashing below. Earl went down to one knee, holding his chest in pain. After finally catching his breath, the old man went over to the shattered window and looked below, only to find nothing but broken glass on the ground.

15 April 1864

I am not sure what to make of all the strange stories and rumors regarding the missing women and children. It appears as if they suddenly vanished into thin air. Some openly declare that Yankee spies are responsible, while others secretly believe it is something more sinister. I fear it is the latter. My dear friend, Martha Benson, swears that she saw an evil face staring at her through her bedroom window just the other night.

The war has gone on far longer than anyone imagined. Oh, how I do miss my dear Robert.

From the diary of Charlotte Jennings
April 15, 1864

TEN

Crown Manufacturing, located near Montgomery, was the main employer for most of the residents in Plainridge. At 7:00 a.m. Buzz Jenkins, first shift foreman, kicked open the door of the employee break room and shouted, "Has anyone seen George Sikes? He's late again. If he ain't here in five minutes, he's fired!"

***

Later that morning, Greg was awakened by the continuous ringing of his phone next to his bed. It had been a long night. He had stayed with Rachel until she had fallen asleep. Then after checking all the locks and covering each window, he retreated back to his apartment, exhausted from the previous day.

"Uh, hmmm . . . hello?" Greg said, lying on his right side with his eyes still closed and the phone in his ear.

"Greg, it's Earl, did I wake you up?"

"Yeah, but I'm glad you called. Rachel told me something interesting last night. I think Loretta's moving around a lot."

"Oh, I know she is, 'cause I ran into her," Earl responded.

Greg could tell that he'd been up most of the night because his old voice sounded more raspy than usual. Greg sat up on the edge of his bed. "Where?" Greg asked.

"At John Hayes' house."

"Earl, what were you doing up there?" Greg said as he began putting on his blue jeans and red hoodie sweatshirt.

"You need to get dressed and come over and I'll show you," Earl replied.

"I'll be there in a little bit."

***

At 10:00 a.m., George Sikes began relentlessly pounding on the front door of Joe's Pub & Grill. After several moments, a voice from behind the door began yelling, "HOLD ON, HOLD ON, I'M COMIN'." That didn't stop George Sikes from continuing to pound on the door. "HOLD ON, I SAID!"

Joe Skinner jerked the metal door wide open and stared at George in disbelief. "George, what the heck are you doin' here? You know we don't open 'til two o'clock," Skinner said, standing in the doorway wiping his hands on the white apron around his waist.

He paused for a moment, tilting his bald head, while giving George a suspicious look. "Why ain't you at work?" George Sikes lowered his eyes, mumbled a few incoherent words, and stumbled into the bar, knocking Skinner to one side. He made his way over to his favorite stool at the end of the counter and collapsed, placing his head on the bar.

Skinner could tell he wasn't feeling well. The normally dark, complicated man looked ghostly white and frail. "Heck, I know it's early, but how 'bout a drink, George? It's on the house," Skinner stated, making his way back behind the bar. He then walked over and placed the drink in front of George Sikes, who continued to be face down on the counter. "George, you don't look too good. Maybe you need to go see Doc Covin?"

George Sikes didn't utter a word, but looked up at his drink, grabbed it with his right hand, and took a hard swallow, which he immediately spewed out of his mouth and onto Skinner. "HEY! WHAT'S THE BIG IDEA?" Skinner screamed, using his apron to wipe off his face. There was no answer. George abruptly stood up and with a strange and distant look across his pale face, staggered out the front door and to his truck.

Skinner quickly ran over, locked the front door, and studied George Sikes from the window. He erratically spun his truck out of the gravel parking lot back onto Taylor Street. Skinner walked back to his small, private office in the back, picked up the phone, and dialed the county courthouse.

"Sheriff's department, this is Susie."

"Susie, this Joe Skinner; is Deputy Sims around?"

"Yes sir, let me transfer you to his office."

***

Greg Jones slammed on his brakes as he approached the curb next to Earl's house. Earl had intentionally left the front door open for him. As Greg raced up the front steps, he could see through the screen door directly into Earl's den. The old man was sitting on the floor with papers spread out in front of him. The worn screen door made a high-pitch squeak when Greg opened it and walked in.

"What are you doin' on the floor?" Greg asked. Earl slowly pulled himself up off the floor and awkwardly made his way over to Greg, while rubbing his stiff neck. His thick, gray hair was a tangled mess, and deep, dark circles engulfed the area beneath his eyes.

"Want some coffee?" Earl asked, stretching his back out.

"Sure. What's with all the papers on the floor?"

"I couldn't sleep last night after what the widow Crenshaw told us," Earl replied while pouring hot coffee into a couple of mugs. "All the way home last night, I kept wondering if any of my ancestors were at that secret meeting and why my daddy had never mentioned it or if he even knew about it." Earl walked over, handed Greg a mug, and they both walked into the den. "As I was lying in bed last night, it suddenly occurred to me that John Hayes probably had some information about the history of the town. I know, as a descendant of Dorothy Lee, he at least had her diary in his house. So I decided to get what I could before Deputy Sims and Mayor Watson cleaned out his house."

"What did you find?" Greg asked, leaning forward to study some of the papers on the floor.

"Well, I found the town charter the widow referred to and some other interesting newspaper clippings, diaries, and other information that date back before the Civil War. I've been up all night reading. I can't put it down."

"Were you able to tell if any of your ancestors were involved?" Greg asked.

Earl got up from his recliner and gently picked up the town charter. He sat down next to Greg on the sofa. "Not that I could tell," Earl stated as he slowly rolled out the charter for Greg to see. "I've studied my family tree, and I don't recognize any of these names, except for Dorothy Lee and Hester Lynch."

Greg placed his coffee mug on the table next to the sofa and began reading the old document. He placed his hand over his mouth in disgust at what he was reading and felt nausea rolling in his gut. He then noticed at the bottom that the names were signed in what looked like dark brown ink. He suddenly recalled the widow saying that the new charter had been signed in blood. He quickly withdrew his hand from the document. "Earl, can you believe they actually did this?"

"I think it explains why our town is cursed," Earl replied. "There are references about Hester Lynch and the secret meeting in Dorothy Lee's diary, but this is the only document that reveals what actually happened at that meeting."

"How did he do it? I mean, how did Hester Lynch convince these people to sign this charter?"

"That's a good question. As I read through Dorothy Lee's diary, I got the impression that most folks feared him and didn't want to cross him. Greg, I think it goes even deeper than that. I've always believed that when people are confronted with a hardship or difficulty, they either turn to the Lord or away from Him."

"What about Loretta? You mentioned you saw her again," Greg said.

"As I was reading the town charter on John's bedroom floor, I heard a strange noise downstairs. The next thing I know, she's standing in the doorway staring at me. Greg, I didn't recognize her. All I saw was pure evil. I could feel its hatred for me. I was so frightened; it reminded me of last October when we saw Hester Lynch in that rocking chair. In that brief moment as we faced each other just a few feet apart, it occurred to me that I wasn't really looking at Loretta Sikes, but an evil spirit personified."

"What happened?"

Earl closed his eyes and placed his head into his open hands as he began reliving the nightmare all over again. "I found myself lying on the floor, my back up against the wall. My chest hurt just staring at her evil face, and then I remembered the cross in my jacket pocket. I grabbed the cross from my pocket and held it up to her. In Jesus' name, I commanded it to leave. Greg, as think back on it, I don't think it was so much the cross I was holding, but I think it saw Jesus inside me because when I mentioned His name, she hissed at me, then turned and jumped out the bedroom window. When I looked out the window, she was gone. I grabbed all the documents and rushed to my truck. I didn't know if I'd make it out alive. I know it was foolish, but I had to find those documents."

"What about the sheriff?" Greg asked. "Was his body still lying on the porch?"

"No, it was gone along with all the broken glass and blood. They cleaned it up pretty good, just like I knew they would. They must've not had enough time to go inside and get his personal belongings."

Greg got up off the sofa and casually walked over to the fireplace. Earl could tell he was in deep thought. "Earl, what exactly did Loretta, or whatever that was, look like?"

"Her face was ghostly white and her eyes were black, void of any signs of life. She was wearing an old ragged dress. I could see her fangs and dried blood around her mouth. She'd looked like she had just crawled out of the earth. Why do you ask?"

"When I went to see Rachel last night, she showed me a picture drawn by a little girl at school. It shook Rachel up pretty bad. The picture was a woman with long, black hair, fangs, and an evil, ghostly white face. Rachel asked the little girl who the picture was supposed to be and the little girl told her that it was the woman who stares at her through her bedroom window every night."

When Earl heard those words, all the color instantly left his face. He looked at Greg in disbelief. "Greg, I think it's time that we go see Mayor Watson. The town's in grave danger. We know it's a spiritual struggle."

"What about Reverend Wilson? He needs to lead this," Greg said.

"Good luck with that," Earl replied, rolling his eyes. "Knowing him, he won't get involved in any type of controversy."

"I don't know why, but the former youth pastor keeps coming into my mind," Greg said, pacing back and forth between the fireplace and couch.

"Scott Evans?" Earl asked.

"Yeah, that's his name. Earl, do you know why he left Plainridge?"

"Well for one, he was an outsider and was never accepted here. I also heard that he and Reverend Wilson didn't get along too good."

"Do you know where he went?" Greg asked.

"Seems like I heard he's at a small Methodist church in Bar Harbor, Maine."

With his hand underneath his chin, Greg stopped pacing and stared out Earl's front window, in deep thought. "Hmmm . . ." Greg pondered out loud, watching the red and yellow autumn leaves blow across the front lawn. "That's a long way from here. Do you think he was trying to get as far away from Plainridge as possible?

"Sounds like it," Earl said as he let out a long yawn and stretched his arms up toward the ceiling.

"I think I'm gonna look him up and give 'im a call," Greg said, looking back at Earl.

"I think I'm going to bed," the old man stated, making his way up off the couch and toward his bedroom. "I'll call you later and we'll go see Mayor Watson tonight. Will Cory come with you?"

"No, he's got class tonight at the junior college. It'll just be us."

ELEVEN

L ater that afternoon, Greg sat alone at his small kitchen table inside his cramped two-room apartment. He had been searching the Internet for Methodist churches in Bar Harbor, Maine. Only five churches had come up on the original search. The first two churches, Prospect Harbor United Methodist and Stonington Methodist, had both come up empty. It was the third choice where he finally found him. Earl was right; he had moved to Maine and was now the youth pastor at the Bar Harbor United Methodist Church. Greg clicked on the church's website and found their main number.

What am I gonna ask him? Greg wondered. *He doesn't know me. I wonder if he'll even talk to me about his time here in Plainridge?* Greg scratched the whiskers on his cheek and raked his hands through his thick, brown hair. Finally, he worked up the courage to pick up the phone. "Guess there's only one way to find out."

Greg grabbed the phone and dialed the church's number.

He was greeted by a friendly voice with a thick, New England accent. "Good afternoon, Bah Habah Methodist Church."

Greg chuckled underneath his breath when he heard the woman's accent. "Yes, I'm looking for Scott Evans."

"You must be a friend or relative of Scott's. I can tell you're from the South," the church receptionist replied.

"I guess you could say friend. Is Scott available?"

"I'll transfer you to his office."

Wow, he's got his own office, Greg thought. *Maybe he just took a better job?*

"Scott Evans."

"Yeah, uh, umm . . . Scott?" Greg was having a hard time collecting his thoughts.

"Yeah, this is Scott."

"Scott, my name is Greg Jones, and I'm the youth pastor here in Plainridge. I was hired after you left. I know we've never met, but if you've got a minute, I was wondering if I could ask you a couple of questions."

Nothing but silence came from the other end. Greg pressed his ear against the phone. "Hello . . . Scott, you there?"

Slowly and in a low voice Scott Evans spoke. "How'd you get this number, and why are you calling me?"

Greg clearly detected an icy tone from his deep Southern accent. He had hit a nerve. A boundary was being put up. "Well, as I said, I'm the youth pastor here in Plainridge, and I came in after you left. A member of our church told me that you had moved to Maine and was the youth pastor at a Methodist church up there. I was hoping you could help me with a few things," Greg replied.

"How much do you know about the town?" Scott asked in a direct, no-nonsense tone.

"More than I knew this time last year," Greg replied, being somewhat coy. He was trying to get as much information from Scott as possible without revealing all that he knew.

"Can you tell the town's spiritually dead?"

"Oh yeah," Greg replied. "I picked up on that pretty early. There's a real secular mindset here, which is really unusual in the South, wouldn't you agree?"

"It's more than that," Scott quickly countered. For a few seconds, there was silence on both ends of the phone. Greg could hear him breathing.

"What do you mean?" Greg finally asked.

"Look, you seem like a nice guy," Scott replied. "I'm just gonna cut to the chase. Greg, there's something about that town. It's more than just spiritually dead. It's evil. I felt it when I first moved there. It was like there was a dark cloud of oppression around the entire town."

"If you don't mind me asking, why'd you leave?"

"I was asked to leave by Reverend Wilson," Scott replied. "Actually, 'asked' is a nice way to put it. He fired me."

"Can you tell me why?" Greg asked, hoping he hadn't overstepped his boundary.

"After several months of barely getting any kids to show up for our youth services, I felt like the Lord put it on my heart to start praying for the town, specifically, for the deliverance of the town. One afternoon, I went to Reverend Wilson and shared with him what the Lord had put on my heart and that I thought he and I should start praying for Plainridge."

"What did he say?" Greg asked.

"Oh, I've never seen a man get so angry. His entire head turned red, like he was about to explode. Then he went off on me. He called me every name in the book. Fundamentalist, narrow-minded fascist, moron, you name it. He told me that there was nothing wrong with their quaint little town, and he wouldn't allow some evangelical nut to ruin it."

"What happened next?" Greg asked, not believing what he was hearing.

"He told me that as far as he was concerned, this conversation never happened and if I brought it up again, I'd be fired. After that, he stood up and stormed out of the church and back to his parish."

"What did you do after that?' Greg asked, leaning forward in his chair.

"Initially, I thought about dropping it, but the Lord kept putting the town on my heart. So I decided to start praying for the town. It was at that point that our relationship turned worse."

"What happened?"

"From that point forward, our relationship was very tense. I felt like he was watching everything I did. He was always angry and volatile. Everything I said and did was wrong. I remember one day, as we were discussing his sermon from the previous Sunday, he leaned back in his chair and asked me if I really believed everything in the Bible. Of course, I said yes. Then he responded by saying, 'Well that's the difference between me and you. I don't take the Bible literally and you do. That's why we can't work together.'"

"Wow!"

"Yeah, I know," Scott replied. "He went on to say that Jesus was basically a good man and there was a lot we could learn from His life, but the idea that He was somehow the Son of God born of a virgin, died on the cross for our sins, and rose from the dead was all just a legend kept alive all these centuries."

"Really, he said that?" Greg asked.

"Greg, you've never picked up on any of this?"

"Well, believe it not, we go weeks without even talking. He spends most of his time inside his parish. I will say though, his sermons are very general in nature and he rarely uses scripture. I remember when I first moved back here, I casually mentioned the spiritual state of the town, and he quickly dismissed it. I could tell that I'd hit a nerve. Anyway, what happened after that?"

Scott paused for a moment before continuing. "I decided that I would obey the Lord and take my chances. So I asked a friend of mine, who was a youth pastor in another town, to come and speak to our youth group. I wanted all the kids in town to show up, so I advertised free pizza. I kept the agenda and the name of the speaker to myself. Let me tell ya, it was an amazing service. After my friend spoke, several kids accepted Christ."

"That's awesome!" Greg replied.

"I know and I don't regret it. The next morning, I got the call from Reverend Wilson."

"What did he say?"

"He basically cussed me out for several minutes, and then told me that I was done at Plainridge Baptist. At that point, I began looking for another job."

"Scott, I really appreciate you telling me this. Do you have any advice for me?"

"Yeah, get out of that town while you can. I can't prove it, but I've always felt that there was some type of dark secret the town was hiding."

"I can't leave," Greg replied as he exhaled. "I haven't been totally honest with you. I'm originally from Plainridge. I came back because it was the only job I could get after college. Also, my fiancée lives here, but there's even a deeper reason why I can't leave." Greg took another deep breath and let it out before continuing. "I feel like the Lord has given me your work to finish."

"I understand," Scott replied. "I gotta verse for you. Greg, are you familiar with 2 Chronicles 7:14?"

"I'm not sure."

"Look it up. It's for you. I gotta go now. Oh, there's one more thing. Greg, have you ever noticed there aren't any crosses anywhere inside or outside the church?" Greg didn't respond, but knew what he was implying. He decided to stay silent. Finally, Scott spoke. "I'll pray for your protection and for Plainridge. Good-bye."

Greg stood up and with both hands on his hips, stretched his back out. That was more than he had expected.

He then walked over and grabbed his Bible off the sofa, flipped to 2 Chronicles 7:14, and began to read it out loud: "If My people who are called by My name humble themselves, and pray and seek My face, and turn from their wicked ways, then I will hear from heaven, and will forgive their sin and heal their land."*

***

Four hours later, Ed Watson was still sitting in his favorite spot in his spacious 1970s-style living room, stroking his large, reddish blond mustache. The living room was located at the front of the house and Watson had already pulled the bright yellow curtains across the windows. His wife knew that this was his favorite place to go when he wanted to be alone and think. He was still reeling from the events that had occurred over the last few days. As a lifelong resident, he knew all about the history and stories surrounding the town. He remembered when he was a boy, watching his father nail a cross to the front door of their home, and then helping him board the windows up with sheets of plywood. The rumor at school was that an entire family in nearby Pickens County had vanished from their farm. He could still vividly recall seeing the FBI men in dark suits and black, horned-rim glasses roaming through the town, interviewing people as to the whereabouts of the missing family. They were Yankees from Washington DC sent by J. Edgar Hoover, and they weren't welcome here. They never found the family or their bodies, but they had to

---

* Scripture taken from the New King James Version

suspect there was a connection with all the crosses and boarded-up windows that suddenly sprang up around town.

Then there was last year, the call from Sheriff Hayes and the story about what had just occurred at the Lynch house with Loretta Sikes. The mayor shifted his position in the bright yellow loveseat and crossed his legs. His thoughts drifted back to that cool autumn day as a ten-year-old boy, asking his father why everyone was boarding up their windows. Watson's father, who was a broad, strong man, looked down at him and with a concerned face said, "Eddie, if you don't bother it, it won't bother you. Like the preacher said, 'If ya talk about it, it'll come looking for ya.' We just gonna stay inside 'til it's over. We ain't gettin' involved."

He was startled by the strong knock on the front door. "I got it honey," Ed yelled, making his way to the front door. He was surprised to see Earl and Greg standing on his front porch. They had noticed the wooden cross nailed to his door and gave each other a confident look as if they knew their timing was perfect.

"Mayor, may we have a word with you?"

"I suppose, come on in," Ed replied. "Have a seat; can I offer you something to drink?"

"No thank you. Mayor, I think we should get right to the point," Earl stated, taking a seat next to the mayor on the loveseat. "I know you and Sheriff Hayes were close friends and . . ."

"Yes we were," Watson jumped in, interrupting Earl. "It's a shame about his passing. He was a dear friend. The funeral service is tomorrow at two o'clock. You know it was a heart attack?"

"Heart attack, huh?" Earl replied, looking over his glasses at the mayor with a look that said "I know you're lying."

"Uh, yeah, um . . ." Watson cleared his throat. "Jim Akins did an extensive autopsy and that was his conclusion."

"I guess it wouldn't have anything to do with his throat being ripped out?" Earl replied, trying to gauge the mayor's reaction.

That caught his attention. "How'd you know?"

Greg jumped in, "Look, Mayor, let's quit playing games. I think we all know that our town's in grave danger. You and your family are in danger." Watson didn't respond, but leaned forward wriggling his sweaty hands together and staring at the floor. Greg continued. "Mayor, we've seen Loretta Sikes. We believe she's responsible for the missing students and the sheriff."

Ed Watson finally looked up, cleared his throat, and carefully chose his words. "Daddy once told me to never talk about that evil thing in those woods off County Road 10. We just put a cross on the door, boarded up the windows, and stayed inside till morning. He said if you don't bother it, it won't bother you." There was a brief pause as he gathered his thoughts. "It was this time last year, when I got the call from John. He told me to meet him at the funeral home, that it was urgent. I immediately got in my car and drove over to Akins' funeral home. When I got there, Jim and John were in the back, looking at Loretta's body."

There was another long pause. Greg could tell this was hard for him to talk about. He continued in a somber tone. "John assured us that he would handle it. He was going to bury her along with all the town's past sins and secrets in a grave at the back of Asbury. We made a promise to each other never to discuss this with anyone. Then George Sikes started running his mouth around town, tellin' anyone who'd listen that he'd seen her."

"Ed," Earl began while placing his hand on the mayor's back in an effort to comfort him, "I wish getting rid of our sins was that easy, but it's not. I know you think putting that cross on your front door will save you, but it won't. Only Jesus can save you and protect you from the evil one. The Bible says, 'greater is he that is in you, than he that is in this world.'* Ed, do you know what that means?"

Ed Watson didn't respond, but simply shook his head. Earl and Greg could tell his heart was troubled. Earl continued, "Ed, it means that we're in a war between God and Satan. It's a war that's being going on a long time, but the good news is that Jesus won the war when He died on the cross and rose from the grave. When a person asks Jesus to forgive them and become their Lord and Savior, He does more than just forgive their sins; He comes to live inside them, and He protects them from the evil one. He begins to change that person from the inside out. The good news doesn't stop there. When they die, their spirit is pardoned by God, and they get to live with Him forever. I know your daddy told you to just leave evil alone and it would leave you

---

* Scripture taken from the King James Version

alone, but that's not the way it works. The Bible says in 1 Peter that your adversary, the devil, roams around like a roaring lion seeking whom he may devour. Ed, there's no neutral ground in this war. You have to choose a side. No decision—is a decision. This town chose its master a long time ago, and we've been paying for it ever since, but that doesn't have to be the final story. The Lord loves everyone in this town, and He wants to make it new."

That last sentence caught his attention. Watson adjusted his bifocals and stroked his mustache again while looking directly at Earl and Greg. "You've given me a lot to think about it," Watson stated. "Thanks for coming by." As the men stood up and shook hands, Earl decided to add one more thing.

"Ed, as mayor, in the interest of protecting the citizens of this town, I think you should impose a curfew at dusk starting tomorrow."

"Don't you think that'll scare everyone?" Watson asked.

With one eyebrow raised, Earl looked at Ed over the top of his glasses and said sternly, "I think the town's expecting it."

On that note, Ed Watson thanked the men for stopping by and quickly ushered out them out the front door, locking it behind them. He was numb from exhaustion, but continued to pace back and forth in the dimly lit living room. The aging mayor found himself at a personal crossroads. He was wrestling between what he had always believed versus the new information he had received that night. Deep down, he knew what Earl had told him was the truth, but he was struggling with the courage to take the next step. He had a sick feeling in the pit of his stomach and all of a sudden, it felt like the weight of the world was on his shoulders. He was startled when his wife, hair in curlers, popped into the living room with horror wretched across her face.

"Honey, sorry to bother you. I know you like being alone when you come in here, but I just got off the phone with Ruth and she told me that the Bagwell's baby is missing. According to Ruth, Maggie Bagwell went into the baby's room to check on her and the crib was empty. The window behind the baby's crib was open. Folks could hear her screaming all the way down the street."

"I hadn't heard. I was talking with Earl Smith and Greg Jones. I'll call Deputy Sims right now to see if it's been reported."

"Well, Ruth said it's all over town. People are starting to gather at their house."

As soon as his wife left the room, Ed Watson dropped to his knees next to the loveseat. Fear and conviction had his heart clamped in a strong vice grip. Everything he had always believed and trusted was vanishing before his very eyes. He began to realize that control was merely an illusion, and he was a just a helpless old man. Even though he attended church every Sunday, he had never been a praying man and for most of his life, even questioned the existence of God. His hands trembled as he awkwardly put them together. He started off slowly, "Lord,

I don't know where to begin. I guess I've never given You Your due, but somehow I know You're real. Jesus, I believe You died for my sins. I'm sorry for all my sins; please forgive me and save me. I want to know You. I want to know the truth. Lord, I'm scared. Please help me. Amen."

TWELVE

OCTOBER 30TH

The next morning, the residents of Plainridge were awakened by the PA system on top of Deputy Sims' patrol car. His distinct country accent was coming through loud and clear. "Citizens of Plainridge, for your safety, a curfew will be imposed starting this evening at dusk. All violators will be arrested. Thank you for your cooperation."

Not all citizens were caught off guard. Several people had already begun boarding up their windows and placing crosses on their front doors. Just a block down from Main Street, Edgar Winters had just finished boarding up one window and was getting ready to start on the next one. He felt euphoric that it was still morning, and he was already ahead of several of his neighbors. One street over, on Taylor Street, Joe Skinner was in the process of trying to hang a heavy wooden cross to the steel door of his pub, while just a couple of businesses down, Doyle Higgins was attempting to build a large cross by welding two pieces of scrap metal together. Word had spread quickly about the Bagwell's baby and most began to suspect there was a connection between the three missing lacrosse players, the sheriff's death, and the missing baby. Evil had been unleashed on the town and the residents were bracing for the storm they knew was coming.

Greg's tan jeep sped down Main Street on his way to the library. He wanted to take another look at some of the old pictures of Crossville prior to the Civil War and in particular, October 1954, when a family in nearby Pickens County had suddenly vanished. As he watched the busy activity around town, he could sense the fear and anxiety. No one was going to work today, that was for sure. Instead, they had made the decision to call in sick and feverishly work on their homes and places of business, trying to get everything done before sunset.

He was troubled by a text he had received from Rachel earlier that morning, letting him know that the principal had asked her to stay late and make sure the school was closed and locked up before she left. He had sent her a text back about the curfew, but she hadn't responded. She usually stayed past four o'clock grading papers and getting organized for the next day, but Greg knew by the time it would take her to do her normal work and check each window and door throughout the school, it would be getting dark and tonight was not the night to be coming home after dark.

Why would Principal Morgan ask Rachel to stay late and make sure the school was locked up? He's never done that before, Greg thought as he pulled up next to the curb in front of the public library. Then it hit him. *Because Greg, he wants to be home before dark. Coward!* Greg sat in his parked jeep, thinking; anger starting building up inside of him. *Morgan's always had it out for her, just because she's an outsider.* He decided that he would head over to the school after Sheriff Hayes' funeral service and help her get everything locked up.

With Earl at home, Greg knew no one would be in the library, and he could study the old photos in private. As he stepped off the street and onto the sidewalk, he was startled by Luther Dickens flying down Main Street, dangerously close to the curb, in an old beat-up truck loaded down with plywood. He could tell that no one, including Deputy Sims, was worried about things like speed limits or traffic violations. Right now, time was of the essence and it was every person for himself.

Greg entered the dark, musty library and began searching for the lights. He shuddered while trying to warm his hands with warm air from his mouth. He could tell the heat hadn't been turned on in a while and the old library felt more like a meat locker than a public library. After finding the light switch and thermostat, he immediately walked down the steps to the main floor and headed to the table in the back. He thought about last year when Earl had grabbed one of the books off the table to show Cory an old photo of Hester Lynch.

Using his right hand, Greg wiped a layer of dust off the first book he found and began flipping through it. There was nothing unusual about this photo album, just a collection of old mundane pictures of the town in the 1950s. However, his attention was drawn to an old newspaper turned sideways in the very back of the album, like someone had just read it and quickly stuffed it back in. Greg unfolded

the brown, crisp, faded newspaper and read the headline and
date out loud.

THE MONTGOMERY ADVERTISER,
WEDNESDAY, OCTOBER 25, 1954:

Federal Authorities Investigate Disappearance
of Pickens County Family
By G. H. Lumpkin

Federal agents arrived in Montgomery
yesterday to continue the search for the
missing Pickens County family. According
to several unnamed sources, Vernon
Johnson, his wife, and two children
mysteriously vanished from their rural farm
over a week ago. Local authorities
conducted an area wide search but found no
evidence of foul play.

Upon hearing of the strange occurrence, the
head of the Federal Bureau of Investigation,
J. Edgar Hoover, has sent a team of agents
to open a new investigation into the matter.
According to several sources, the search has
moved from Pickens County to the small
remote town of Crossville.

On the front page of the paper were pictures of G-men in black suits, white shirts, skinny black ties, and horned-rim glasses walking down Main Street. Greg could tell that the town hadn't changed much since then. As he looked at the picture closer, something caught his eye in the background.

Just behind one of the FBI agents, Greg could clearly see a boarded-up window with a large cross nailed to the front. He immediately recognized the building. It was Moore's Hardware, just a few yards from where he was standing. He remembered the story Earl had told him about the family that disappeared and not a trace of them was ever found. Suddenly, the image of the skulls and bones stacked in the cellar at the Lynch house came to his mind, and he couldn't help but wonder if some of those bones had belonged to the missing family.

Greg walked over and sat down at one of the center tables and decided to call Earl. He had been halfway expecting him to walk through the doors at any moment, but found it odd he hadn't shown up. The phone rang several times before the old man finally answered. Greg could tell he wasn't feeling well. His old voice sounded weak.

"Earl, it's Greg. Did I wake you up?"

"No Greg, I'm just under the weather. Actually, I don't feel good at all. It must've been gettin' out in the cold the other night. I don't think I'm gonna be able to make it to the funeral service today."

"Is there anything you need?" Greg was concerned.

"Naw, just some rest," Earl replied.

"There's a curfew starting at dusk."

"I heard. Greg we need pray for our town and for God's protection. Please promise me that you'll take the curfew seriously."

"I will and I'll call you later, okay?"

"Sounds good. I'll talk with you later. Good-bye."

Before Greg could say good-bye, his phone lit up. It was Cory. "Hey Cory, what's up?"

"Greg, have you heard about the Bagwell's baby?"

"What are you talkin' about?" Greg asked, sitting straight up in his chair.

"It's all over town, Greg. Maggie Bagwell went in to check on her baby before going to bed, but the baby was gone, snatched from its crib. The Bagwells can't be consoled right now. Greg, if she was at the sheriff's house two nights ago and the Bagwell's last night, then—"

"Then she could be anywhere in town." Greg sat momentarily with his hand covering his mouth. *No wonder people were panicking. This has to end.*

"Greg, you there?" Cory asked.

"Yeah, you goin' to the funeral today?"

"Yeah, I'll meet ya there a little before two," Cory responded. "After that, I've gotta head to my class in Montgomery."

"Okay, I'll see you at the church," Greg replied.

***

At 1:45 p.m., most of the town's residents had gathered at the church to pay their last respects to Sheriff

John Hayes. Most folks had finished the preparations to their homes and just had a few things to do before they retired inside before sunset. Greg saw Cory's tall frame standing out front, his shoulder-length blond hair blowing in the wind. He pulled his jeep into his usual parking place in front of the church and got out.

The rumor from those still mingling out front was that there would be no graveside service, just a quick, private, burial later this afternoon. Greg thought it was ironic that just less than a year ago the sheriff, along with Jim Akin, had ordered the same type of service for Loretta. Just moments before the beginning of the service, he and Cory squeezed into the small, white, colonial-style church and stood in the back. The pews were already full and the old church was packed to capacity.

Greg took a moment to scan the crowd and quickly noticed that very few people seemed upset. It seemed surreal that there wasn't any crying or grieving. Instead, most people kept looking at their watches, as if they were ready for the service to be over with. It seemed more like a church meeting than a funeral. A sudden gust of strong autumn wind caught Greg's attention and temporarily captured his focus. As he looked through one of the large, colorful stained-glass windows, he found himself studying the town's oldest oak tree, which hovered above the church like a large spider. Its old, thick arms blocked out much of the afternoon sun as its colorful leaves were being scattered in every direction. Greg began to imagine Reverend Silas in a traditional black suit and white shirt, hanging from the tallest limb with the rope still tight against his neck, his slowly decaying corpse and swollen, bulging eyes staring back at him through the window. *Stop it!* he reprimanded himself and refocused his attention up front.

At exactly two o'clock, the heavyset, gray-haired Reverend Wilson emerged from the side door and walked to the pulpit. Dressed in his traditional black suit, he seemed at ease and even let out a few smiles as he welcomed and thanked everyone for coming. Looking over the top of the crowd, Greg could see John Hayes' pale face lying peacefully in the coffin, his hands placed neatly across his chest.

"Good afternoon," Wilson's thunderous voice echoed through the congregation. "I want to thank everyone for coming today, and I know John would certainly appreciate everyone stopping by to pay their last respects and to say good-bye to their old friend. Like many of you here, John and I go way back. We grew up together here in Plainridge and shared a lot of good memories. I know we'll all miss seeing John around town. I know I speak for everyone when I say, how safe we all felt seeing his patrol car cruising around town. He was committed to keeping our town safe and keeping outsiders away."

The last sentence caught Greg's attention, *That was weird,* he thought. Wilson continued. "We all know the last couple of years were hard on John after losing Emily and if it comforts you, you can believe they're together again. However, if you don't believe in that sort of thing, that's okay too. That's what makes our town so special. We don't force certain religious beliefs on each other. That's the way John would've wanted it.

"So in closing, I'd just like to say we're all going to miss you, John. If you haven't had a chance to stop by the coffin to say your good-byes we'll be here for another thirty minutes or so. Our new sheriff, Sheriff Sims . . . sorry it's going to take a little while to get use to saying that," Wilson chuckled while giving a glance over to Sims who was sitting nervously on the front row, "has asked that I remind y'all about the curfew at dusk tonight. In light of that, there won't be a graveside service, just a private burial later this afternoon. Thank you again for coming and please keep the missing students and their families in your prayers. Have a nice afternoon."

Have nice afternoon? Was this a funeral or church meeting? Greg wondered. He noticed that the church was clearing out fairly quickly, and with only a few hours of daylight left, folks had apparently decided to get back to their homes. He carefully observed the reverend talking with the new sheriff next to the casket and decided it was now time to have that one-on-one talk.

"Cory, I'll catch up with you later, I need to say something to Reverend Wilson."

"Okay, Greg, I'll talk with you later."

Greg maneuvered his way through the crowd and toward the front of the church. His eyes stayed glued to Wilson who had just retreated back through the side door and into his office. With a gentle tap on the door, Greg announced his presence.

"Reverend, can I have just a minute of your time?"

Wilson looked up with a piercing stare. His eyes were dark and cold and shot a hole right through Greg. "All I got's a minute; I've got a private graveyard service to attend. How can I help you?"

"Reverend, it was just something you said out there that bothered me."

"What was that?" Wilson replied in a snippy tone, while giving Greg a stern look like "you better watch your step."

"It was what you said about the hereafter and its okay to believe what you want and all that. It just bothered me. Shouldn't we be telling people about salvation through Christ alone and that He is the only way to eternal life?"

Wilson's facial color changed rapidly from pale to beat red. He crossed his arms and stared at Greg with his narrow, cold eyes. Finally he spoke. "Greg, you remind me a lot of your predecessor, Scott Evans. He had the same judgmental, narrow-minded philosophy that you do. You know what happened to him, don't you?"

Judgmental? Greg couldn't believe what he was hearing. He simply responded by nodding his head.

"Good. If you ever mention this again to me or anyone in this town, you'll find yourself with the same fate. Do we understand each other?"

Again, Greg nodded, while trying not to make eye contact.

"If you'll excuse me, I'm headed to Asbury to conduct a graveside service."

"Greg, that's the problem, I can't find Principal Morgan's keys to lock up. I think he forgot to give them to me."

"Okay, let's just go through the school and make sure all the windows are locked. Then we'll head over to his house, get the keys, and come back and lock the doors," Greg replied in a reassuring tone.

"Okay, let's hurry, it'll be dark soon."

***

George Sikes sat alone at dusk, waiting, his back up against Loretta's headstone. With the final few fleeting moments of daylight left, he pondered if she would come. He barely remembered seeing her the night before last, but since then he couldn't get her out of his mind. He hadn't been to work in a couple of days, but that didn't matter now. Actually, he couldn't remember what he had done or where he had gone. The last couple of days seemed like a blur. He'd lost his appetite. Food no longer tasted good. All he could think about was Loretta.

He thought it was strange that Reverend Wilson had called him out of the blue to come over to Asbury late that afternoon to fill the sheriff's open grave. He didn't even know the sheriff was dead, but the thought of being in Asbury close to Loretta's grave compelled him to come. Now that the sun had completely sat beneath the horizon, he sat still in the dark and listened. Anxiety grew in the pit of his stomach. He heard the occasional rustling of the wind blowing through the trees. Then there it was, the soft sound of footsteps heading his way.

***

Rachel screamed and covered her face as Greg swerved his jeep just in time to barely miss the oncoming car that had veered over into their lane. Greg was driving like a mad man trying to get back to the school. The whole ordeal at Morgan's house had taken longer that he had planned. Initially, they'd had a hard time finding his house and with all the residents reluctant to open their doors, it only slowed the process down.

Finally, they found the principal's home and after talking to him, through his front door, Greg finally managed to convince Morgan to give him his key to the school, even though he only did so by opening the door just enough to toss the key to Greg.

With his jeep lights on bright, Greg quickly turned off Taylor Street and pulled up next to the front door of the school.

"Don't forget about the doors in the very back," Rachel said, just as he was about to get out of the jeep.

Great! Greg thought. He didn't want to walk down the long, dark hallway all the way to the back of the school, but he knew Morgan would blame Rachel if all the doors weren't locked. He also didn't want to leave Rachel by herself in his jeep.

"Hey honey, why don't you come with me? I don't want you sitting out here alone. Grab that flashlight out of the glove compartment."

Rachel got out of the jeep and they both slowly made their way into the dark school. Greg secretly wished he'd brought a cross or gun with him. The hallway was dark and the only visible light came from his flashlight and the light stretching in from the parking lot. Rachel wrapped her arms tight around Greg's waist as the two walked side by side toward the back of the school. Cautiously, they moved forward, shining the flashlight around the corner of each classroom and down the hall.

Finally, and to their relief, they had made their way to the metal door. Greg reached down, pulled the key out of his jeans pocket, and successfully locked the school door. They then turned around and began walking much more quickly down the hall, back toward the front of the school; Greg was ready to get out of there and back home. He hoped they wouldn't be pulled over by Sheriff Sims and arrested for violating curfew.

Halfway down the dark hall, something in the distance caught his eye through a classroom window. "Rachel, stop," he whispered. "I think I see something."

Rachel pulled close to Greg and began to shake. "What is it?"

Greg stood still in the hall, flashlight in his right hand, staring past the open classroom door and out the classroom window. They were on the Asbury side of the school. The cemetery was no more than one hundred yards from where they standing. In the complete darkness, he could clearly see the graveyard at the top of the hill. On the very edge of the cemetery stood a lone, white figure, which seemed to be looking directly at him through the window. Chills rose up his spine. He was too terrified to move. He quickly turned his flashlight off.

"Why'd you turn the flashlight off?" Rachel asked.

"Shhh . . . don't move," Greg whispered.

Rachel squeezed him tighter. "Greg, you're scaring me."

"I think it's her. She must've seen the beam from our flashlight."

"What's she doing?" Rachel asked in a trembling voice. Her body was now shaking uncontrollably.

"She's just staring at us, I think. I'm not sure." There was something else, but Greg was reluctant to mention it. She seemed to be holding some type of round object in her right hand. Greg squinted and focused his eyes. The round object appeared to be dangling by something, then it hit him. *It's a head! She's holding a severed head!* Greg swallowed hard and tried his best to keep his composure.

"Rachel, let's slowly step away from the window, okay?" Rachel nodded, continuing to cling onto Greg. In unison, they both took two slow steps to the right until they were no longer in view of the window. "Rachel, run!"

Rachel let go of Greg's arm, and they raced down the pitch-black hallway until they saw the front door. Greg kicked the door open and quickly turned around to lock it while Rachel ran toward the jeep. Once inside, she immediately locked her door, but she could tell something was wrong. Greg was taking longer than usual; the key had gotten stuck in the lock. She began to scream.

"GREG HURRY! JUST LEAVE IT!" she yelled from inside the jeep. Finally, he managed to get the key out of the lock; he ran toward his jeep and jumped in. Greg got the jeep started and floored the gas pedal, jerking the steering wheel hard to the left, causing the jeep to slide on two wheels across the empty parking lot. Rachel screamed, fearing they were about to crash. Greg managed to regain control of the vehicle and sped onto Taylor Street and back to Rachel's house.

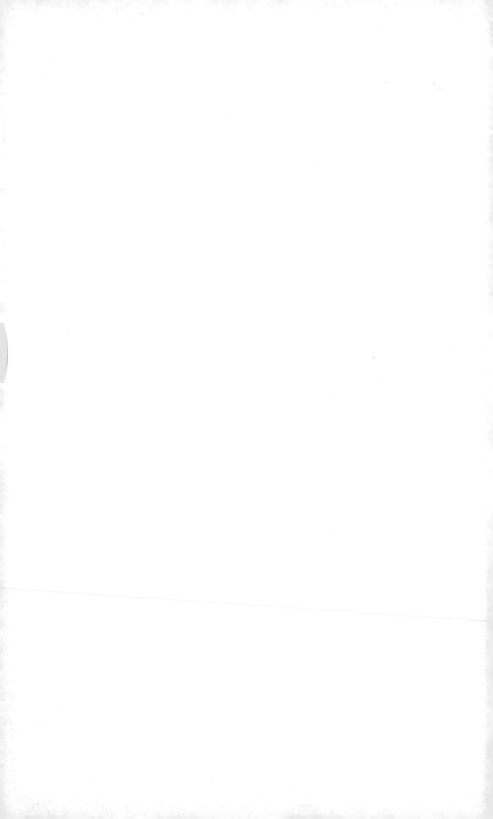

FOURTEEN

Greg didn't bother slowing down as he approached the only red light in town, but instead turned sharply onto Main Street, veering over into the left-hand lane. The town looked like a ghost town. Windows on every building and home were boarded up and there wasn't a soul in sight. "Greg, why are all the windows boarded up?" Rachel asked.

"I think that's what they did like fifty years ago when this sort of thing happened," he casually replied while smiling at her. "I think we're the only ones who didn't get the memo."

"It's happened before?" she asked in a panic. "Greg, are we going to be safe?"

"Honey, I'll lock and cover the windows. If it's okay, I'll stay over and sleep on your couch."

"I wish you would," Rachel replied.

Pulling up to the curb next to Rachel's house, Greg turned his off the engine and stepped out of the jeep. He listened intently, as if he could hear something no one else could. Rachel quickly raced up the steps to her front door.

"Rach, do you hear that?"

"Hear what?" she responded, digging into her purse for her house key. "All I hear is the wind."

"That!" Greg emphatically responded, standing on the second step, again listening with his head angled to one side. "It sounds like a high-pitched scream coming from Asbury." A chill crawled up his spine; he knew they didn't have much time. "Hurry, let's get inside."

Once inside, Greg and Rachel immediately began locking each window and pulling the curtains across the front. Greg found an old newspaper and began frantically taping it to the inside of Rachel's bedroom window.

***

Across town, at Doyle's Auto Repair, Doyle Higgins sat fully dressed in his grease-stained overalls in the back of his garage on the edge of his dirty bed. He had his shotgun across his lap, lights out, listening for any strange sounds. Just a couple of doors down, Joe Skinner calmed his nerves with a cold drink under the flicker of a small candle. Over on Main Street, Ed Watson sat in his favorite spot, next to his wife, reading his Bible. Normally, she left him alone, but not tonight. Even though she thought it was strange, his sudden interest in the Bible, she felt safe being next to him in their dark house.

The same story was being played out simultaneously across the town. Families huddled together in one room in the dark and under candlelight. The goal was simple. Survive the night and pray for daylight. For those who were alive back in 1954, there were stories being told recounting that time, the last time this had happened.

Deep in the back of his funeral parlor, Jim Akin sat with his feet propped up on his desk, taking long draws off the cigarette between his lips. The doors were locked and the lights out front had been turned off hours ago, but he refused to sit in the dark. In his right desk drawer was a .38 Special, fully loaded. Being an agnostic, Akin thought the idea of praying or hanging a cross on the front door of your house or business was complete foolishness, rooted in superstition. He was fully aware of his town's past, including Loretta, but in his mind, there was nothing alive or dead that his thirty-eight couldn't handle.

The short, plump mortician let out a small chuckle to himself and exhaled cigarette smoke from his mouth and nostrils. His thoughts drifted back to the encounter he'd had earlier in the day with his long-time friend, Ed Watson. Akin had wandered, unannounced, into the mayor's office to see what time he was going to head over to the church for the sheriff's funeral service, when he caught Ed reading a Bible. At first, Akin acted like he didn't see it, but when Ed began telling him that he'd had a personal encounter with Jesus Christ, that was enough. *Never in a million years would I have ever thought Ed would become a religious nut. I guess some folks lose it under pressure,* Akin thought, taking another long drag off the cigarette.

"I need some coffee," he mumbled to himself, taking one last draw before putting the cigarette out in the ashtray on his desk. Standing up, Akin turned on the light to the hallway, which led to the kitchen and coffee machine. "All I know is that I'd better get paid for fixing up the sheriff. That was a dang good job I did on such a short notice; couldn't even tell his neck had been ripped apart."

Maybe it was the hall light that got her attention, but with the sound of water running from the kitchen sink and the coffee machine percolating, Akin never heard her coming. The next sound was glass shattering across the linoleum floor as Akin dropped the full coffee pot and slowly backed into up against the kitchen counter. He was frozen in terror at her appearance just a few feet away. The florescent hall light, which he had intended on replacing, was flickering on and off, creating a horrific strobe light effect of her standing in the hallway.

Akin, with his right hand, slowly opened the utensil drawer next to him and without taking his eyes off her, began feeling around for a knife. She stood still seething, studying him, enjoying his fear.

He decided to make the first move; he'd quickly worked it out in his mind. He'd charge and stab her in the heart. One thing was for certain; he wasn't going down without a fight. Sweat trickled down his plump cheeks and into his beard. With the knife concealed in his right hand, he slowly counted to three in his mind. *One . . . two . . . three!* "AHHHHHHHHH!" Akin screamed at the top of his lungs as he charged and lunged at the vampire. She simply stood there waiting for him with her outstretched claws, beckoning him to come to her. Just a couple of feet from the door, the beast grabbed him by the throat, her long, dirty fingernails digging into his esophagus. He tried to scream, but nothing came out. In a matter of a few moments, Jim Akin had drowned in his own blood.

***

At 12:00 a.m., Greg was suddenly awakened by his phone on Rachel's coffee table. He'd gotten Rachel off to bed and had fallen asleep on her couch. His brown hair was matted down on one side and his neck ached from the way he'd slept. "Hello?" It was Earl. He didn't sound right.

"Greg, I . . . know it's . . . not a good time . . . but I need your help." Greg could tell he was struggling, gasping for air.

"Earl, what's wrong?"

"I'm . . . having a hard time . . . breathing. My chest feels real tight. I . . . think I'm having a heart attack. Can you . . . take me to the hospital . . . in Montgomery?"

"I'll be right over; just hang in there," Greg said.

Greg immediately thought about Rachel. *I can't leave her tonight,* was his immediate thought. *Wait a minute, maybe she can go with us to the hospital.* He got up, went to Rachel's room, and woke her up. "Rachel, wake up!"

Startled and still half asleep, Rachel jumped up in bed. "Greg, what's wrong?"

"I just got a call from Earl; he may be having a heart attack. I've got to get him to Montgomery. Rachel, I want you to come with us. I don't want to leave you here alone."

"Greg, I'm exhausted. I've got to get up early for work. Go ahead and take him, I'll be fine."

"Okay, I'll lock the door on my way out, but just call me you if get scared and I'll get Cory to come over and check on you. I love you."

"I love you too," Rachel said, collapsing back into her soft pillow. It wasn't long before she was fast asleep.

FIFTEEN

G reg had the gas pedal all the way to floor and his hazard lights flashing. Earl was lying across the backseat of his jeep, struggling for his next breath. They were headed to University Hospital in Montgomery. He kept one eye on Earl in his rearview mirror and one eye on the road as he weaved his way through the light morning traffic. He knew it was serious when he showed up at Earl's house only to find him lying on the floor. The old man looked pale and his breathing was labored. Greg's mind kept drifting back to Rachel. *Lord, please keep her safe. Please send Your angels to watch over her.*

***

At 2:00 a.m., Rachel suddenly woke up and sat straight up in bed. She began rubbing her eyes, trying her best to determine the time on the alarm clock next to her bed. For some reason, she found herself fully awake. *Greg, I wish you were here.*

Then a strange sound from outside her window caused her to gasp out loud. It was the sound of twigs snapping, the unmistakable sound of footsteps. *Could just be an animal.* Rachel pulled the covers up to her chin and stared at her small bedroom window. The newspaper that Greg had taped to the inside of the window was so thin that it barely kept the moonlight out. Rachel sat still, her eyes fixated on the window.

Then a silhouette of a figure appeared and stood in front of the window. Without thinking, Rachel let out a loud scream. "AHHHH!" She could tell the figure was a woman, about her height, with long hair that draped down her narrow shoulders. Paralyzed by fear, Rachel continued to stare at the window. A moment later, she saw the figure raise its hand up and place it on the window, which was followed by the terrifying sound of *Tap . . . Tap . . . Tap . . .* Then a long *scr-ee-ch* across the cold glass. Rachel let out another loud scream.

Instinctively, she jumped out of bed and ran to her front door. Her survival instincts kicked into full gear. Somehow, she knew that she had to get out of the house. She'd forgotten that she'd left her car at the school. Barefoot and still in her pajamas, she unlocked the front door and raced down the concrete steps only to trip and fall.

She didn't know how long she'd been face down on the sidewalk. She remembered tripping and falling. Her head ached and she felt warm blood running down the side of her face. She tried to get up but couldn't move. Something was wrong with her left leg. Her ears were ringing, but she could faintly hear the shattering of glass coming from inside her house.

Struggling and crawling on her stomach, her left leg dangling behind her, Rachel made a futile attempt to get away. The pain was excruciating. Then behind her, she heard footsteps approaching. *Lord help me.*

"Do not be afraid," were the last words she remembered hearing before passing out.

***

The emergency room at University Hospital was packed with patients with various cases from car accidents to headaches. Fortunately, for Earl, heart-attack patients were pushed to the front of the line. Several hours had passed since they had first arrived at the hospital. Greg sat in the crowded, chaotic waiting room, his head and body leaned up against the wall. He was beyond numb with exhaustion.

Even though he didn't want to wake Rachel up, he felt compelled to call and check on her. He felt the full weight of guilt and remorse for leaving her. It weighed on him like a heavy blanket. Greg pulled his phone out his pocket and dialed her cell number. *Rach, please pick up the phone.* After several rings, and no answer, he remembered her telling him that her battery had died. They'd forgotten to charge it when she got home. *Shoot!*

More troubling than not being able to reach her was something Earl had muttered in the backseat on the way to the hospital. The old man had been rambling incoherently off and on the whole way. Greg assumed it was because he wasn't getting enough oxygen to his brain, but at one point, he leaned up, touched Greg on the arm, and said very plainly, "Greg, the Lord wants you to trust Him completely." *What did that mean?* Greg pondered that question. He closed his eyes and feel into a deep sleep.

He didn't know how long he'd been asleep, when a doctor in green scrubs came and put his hand on his arm. "Mr. Jones?"

"Uh . . . umm . . . yeah?" Greg sat up, his blue flannel shirt was twisted and wrinkled from the way he was sitting.

The doctor sat down next to him. "I'm sorry," he said in a very direct tone.

The words didn't register. Greg was still half asleep. He was trying to wake up, to compose his thoughts. He looked at the doctor, tilted his head, and said, "What do you mean?"

"Mr. Jones, he's gone."

Those words hit Greg like a freight train. "What do you mean, he's gone?"

"Mr. Jones, he had a massive cardiac arrest while we were getting him stable. We tried to resuscitate him, but we were unable. I'm sorry."

"NO!" With his hands to his face, Greg began sobbing uncontrollably. Since the death of his father, Earl had become the main father figure in his life. This couldn't be happening. The physician quietly patted Greg on the back and walked back through the doors of the ER.

Greg sat there for several minutes, tears running down his face. Through the chaos of the crowded emergency room, strangers just stared at him and then went on about their business. He felt so alone. After several minutes, he decided to stand and make his way back home. So many thoughts raced through his head. *If I'd just called an ambulance, would he still be alive? If I'd driven faster, maybe they would've had more time to save him.* The rush of shock and pain flowed through him at once. He just wanted to get back to Rachel.

Just as he was leaving the ER, a nurse came running up behind him, calling his name. "Mr. Jones?" Greg turned, wiping the tears from his eyes.

"Mr. Jones, I was with your friend, Mr. Smith, before his heart attack. He made me promise that I would give you this message." She briefly paused and looked into Greg's eyes. "He said to tell you to trust the Lord completely no matter how bleak the situation seemed. That's all he said. I hope that helps. I'm so sorry."

Greg nodded and thanked her. Then he left the hospital.

SIXTEEN

OCTOBER 31ST

The very tip of the bright morning sun greeted Greg as he raced down County Road 10 back to Plainridge. Fueled by adrenaline, his hands gripped the leather steering wheel tight. The entire trip home had been a gamut of emotions. Grief, fear, and the rush of anxiety had kept him awake all the way back. Now with the emergence of dawn, he knew the danger was over . . . for now. He prayed, "Lord, please let her be safe."

Passing through the town's Gothic stone crosses, Greg made a sharp left onto Main Street. Even though the sunrise had fully vanquished all elements of the previous night, the town remained deadly quiet. In a matter of moments, he pulled up to Rachel's steps. He immediately noticed the front door wide open and blood smeared across the cracked sidewalk. "NOOO!" he screamed, jumping out of his jeep and running up the steps.

His heart was pumping fast. He burst through the open front door. "RACHEL!" he yelled at the top of his lungs. He expected her to emerge any moment from her bedroom, but deep down he knew she wasn't coming. He raced through the den, knocking down a chair, past the kitchen and into her bedroom. He immediately noticed the room was cooler than the rest of her house, and then he saw the shattered glass spilled onto the bedroom floor.

He crumbled to his knees, crushed. Through his deeps sobs, Greg began to cry out to God. "Why didn't You protect her? Why God . . . why? Where are You?" Through his tears, a sliver of hope began to emerge in his mind when he noticed there was no blood inside her house. If there had been an attack, it had occurred outside. *Maybe it's not too late*, he thought. *Maybe somehow she got away? I've got to find her. Asbury!*

Greg pulled himself up off her bedroom floor and frantically ran out the front door, down the cement steps, and to his jeep. Without even looking for any oncoming cars, he did a U-turn in the middle of Main Street and headed in the opposite direction toward Asbury Cemetery. He blew past Sheriff Sims, who was sitting still in his parked patrol car, sipping on a hot cup of coffee, getting ready for his first patrol. Asbury had been the last place he'd seen Loretta; maybe she had returned to her place of rest . . . hopefully alone.

Greg was somewhat relieved to see the newly appointed sheriff's blue lights flashing behind him, but he didn't slow down. Instead, he pressed the accelerator all the way to the floor, pushing his jeep engine up to seventy miles per hour. He was driving like a maniac. Even though it was now morning, he didn't want to be alone in Asbury, especially after just seeing Loretta there the night before. Taking a quick glance in his rearview mirror, Greg began working out a plan. *Maybe Sims can help me look for Rachel. All I gotta do is explain what happened. He'll understand.* Through all of the chaos of the moment, Greg's thoughts flashed back to the previous night when he saw Loretta standing at the edge of the cemetery. *Whose head was she holding?*

By now, the sheriff's white patrol car had swiftly caught up to Greg. Sims was now flashing his headlights on and off in addition to blowing his siren. Greg acted as if he didn't see him as he turned into the open black iron gates of Asbury Cemetery. Greg drove to the middle part of the cemetery, parked, and immediately got of his jeep. Sims came to a screeching halt, just an inch from his bumper, throwing a cloud of dirt and debris into the cool morning air.

The sheriff sprung from his patrol car with one hand on his hip, next to his gun. "DANG IT GREG, WHY DIDN'T YOU STOP?" The skinny sheriff's face was bright red. Greg noticed the steam rising from the wet coffee stain across his lap.

"Sorry, Deputy."

"IT'S SHERIFF NOW!" he hollered back.

"Oh, uh . . . sorry . . . Sheriff. I really need your help," Greg said, exasperated. "I've got a big problem. Rachel's missing."

"And you thought she'd be out here?"

Both men were suddenly startled by a thunderous sound of blackbirds flying overhead. The gangly sheriff almost jumped out of his skin. "Sheriff, you don't understand. I saw Loretta here last night, and I'm worried that she got to Rachel." He knew immediately that he probably shouldn't have said that. Sims began to nervously look around, while at the same time playing dumb, which he wasn't good at.

"Wh-what are y-y-you talkin' 'bout?" Sims asked, nervously. "You-you-you know Loretta's dead."

"Deputy," Greg began to speak again.

"SHERIFF!"

"Sorry, Sheriff . . ." There was a short pause. Greg began rubbing his forehead, trying to collect his thoughts. "Look, I know all about our town's past. I was up at the Lynch house last year and saw Hester Lynch. I drove a stake in his heart. I also know Sheriff Hayes drove Loretta up here, buried her in a grave, and now she or whatever it is has come back to wreak vengeance on our town."

Sims took a couple of steps back, unsnapped his holster, and pulled his pistol out. Surprised, Greg immediately lifted his arms up in the air to try and calm him down. "Sheriff, I can't find Rachel. I just wanted to take a look around to see if she's here. That's all."

"I want you to slowly turn around and put your hands over your head," Sims responded.

"You're arresting me?" Greg asked, not believing that this was actually happening.

Sims slowly cocked his pistol. "Greg, I ain't asking again."

Greg could see the fear in his eyes. He knew not to push it. He knew fear could cause men to do crazy things. Slowly, he turned around, interlocked his hands behind his head, and leaned against his jeep.

Greg noticed a strange round object not more than thirty yards away, next to the large pine tree he'd leaned up against just a few days ago. He focused his eyes closer and gasped in horror at the realization that it was a decapitated head. Sims began frisking him underneath his untucked blue flannel shirt, then down each leg of his jeans. He continued to stare at the head, trying to identify it. From this vantage point, he could see the victim's long, mangled brown hair covered in dried blood, partially covering its pale face. He felt the cold, steel handcuffs lock. Greg jerked and winced in pain as his wrists were bent back awkwardly. "Can I ask a question?"

"What?" Sims responded.

"What I'm I being arrested for?"

"Well, let's see, breaking curfew, speeding, resisting arrest. That should do it," Sims said with a sarcastic grin across his narrow face.

With one hand on Greg's arm and the other on his holster, Sims led the tall, strong youth pastor over to his patrol car and put him in the back. Greg could tell he wasn't comfortable being here. His beady eyes continued to scan the heavily shaded, quiet graveyard. With hands still behind his back, Greg slid over to the right side of the patrol car and continued to stare at the grizzly scene. He could see the face better from this angle. It was familiar; he'd seen that face before. Then it occurred to him, *That's George Sikes! It was his head she was holding in her hand last night.* The thought horrified him and made him nauseous at the same time. Greg felt like he was about to throw up.

"Sheriff, I think I see a severed head over by that pine tree," Greg stated, leaning forward, trying to get the sheriff's attention. The veins in his neck were bulging and his face was turning red. He could feel the handcuffs cutting into his wrist.

"Sure ya do," Sims responded dismissively. "You think I just fell off the turnip truck? I ain't falling for that." Sims reached over and grabbed his emergency radio. "Susie, this is Sheriff Sims. I've got a prisoner I'm bringing in. Would you make sure our cell is open?"

"Yes sir, who's our guest?"

"Greg Jones, our youth pastor. We'll be there shortly."

SEVENTEEN

Everyone in town stopped what they were doing when they heard the siren and saw the flashing blue lights of the sheriff's patrol car pulling up to the curb next to the white courthouse. It appeared that Sims was clearly enjoying his power as the town's new sheriff and wanted to send a message that he wasn't going to put up with any crime in his town.

The small, two-room police department was conveniently located on the first floor of the courthouse. Susie Price, a short, bubbly blond, sat anxiously at the front counter, working her chewing gum, waiting on the sheriff to bring in his new prisoner. Past the wooden counter was an open area surrounded by wood-paneled walls, which were decorated with various forms of wildlife and old photos of the town. There were two square, metal desks in the middle of the room—one occupied by the sheriff and the other for a deputy officer, which was vacant for now. A heavily stained Mr. Coffee pot sat behind the desk along with a half-eaten box of doughnuts. The department's only jail cell, which was rarely occupied, was located around the corner and past the restrooms.

In an effort to make an even more dramatic scene, Sims slowly emerged out of his patrol car, and with a serious look, took a moment to stare at the small crowd that had gathered at the courthouse. With his left hand, he opened the left rear door, while keeping his right hand on his holster, next to his pistol. As Greg leaned forward in the backseat, Sims reached down and grabbed him by his brown denim jacket. "Watch your head," the sheriff warned, helping Greg out of the patrol car.

Greg felt embarrassed, exhausted, and angry all at the same time. He couldn't get Rachel out of his mind. *Is she alive? Will I ever see her again?* He felt so helpless; it was as if God was taking all his options away. In the last twenty-four hours, he'd lost his fiancée, one of his closest friends, and now he was going to jail. Humiliated and scared, he felt the weight of the world upon his shoulders. With one hand firmly attached to Greg's arm, Sims led him past the crowd, through the front doors, and into the police station.

After a quick processing, the sheriff led Greg back to the dirty, empty cell. "Don't I get a phone call?" Greg asked.

"Maybe later," Sims responded, with a smirk across his face as he slammed the steel door closed and locked it.

Greg walked over, sat on the hard cot, and began to sob. He felt so alone and his body ached. He was about to start questioning God again for his predicament, when it suddenly occurred to him that he was only functioning on a couple of hours of sleep. Stress and fatigue all came together at once as he lay down on the narrow cot. His legs felt like they weighed a hundred pounds each. His body was still and in a matter of seconds, he was fast asleep.

Outside on the main floor, Sims had his feet propped up on his desk with an arrogant smile gleaming across his face. He was stunned when he looked up to see Mayor Watson coming through the glass door of the police station. Watson, didn't stop at the counter, but walked right through to the sheriff's cluttered desk. "Why is Greg Jones in a jail cell?" Watson asked sternly, his arms folded across his chest.

Sims was caught off guard. He immediately removed his feet and began fumbling around through his paperwork. "Well, he broke curfew for one thing."

"And how do you know that?" the mayor asked, still glaring at the young, wiry sheriff.

"He 'fessed up to it. He was also speeding, driving recklessly, and resisting arrest. I finally caught him this mornin' in the cemetery. No tellin' what he was up to. He kept rambling on 'bout his girlfriend, you know, the pretty schoolteacher. He kept on sayin' that she was missin'."

The last part caught Ed Watson's attention. "What'd you just say?"

"'Bout the cemetery?" Sims responded, with a confused look on his face.

"No, about his girlfriend, you said she was missing?"

"Yep, that's what he was sayin', but she's probably at school."

"What's his bail?" Watson asked.

"Aww, don't worry 'bout that, Mayor. I already called his boss and told him all 'bout this mornin'. Reverend

Wilson said he'd be down here after lunch to git 'im. From the sound of things, he didn't sound too happy either." Sims took a moment to let out a little chuckle. "Sounds like after today, he'll end up like the fella they had before him."

***

Later that afternoon, Greg was awakened by the rattling of keys against the cell door. He managed to slowly lift his head from the worn pillow. "Aahhh . . ." he moaned, touching his aching head. *What time is it?* He was shocked when glanced down at his watch and saw three o'clock. *I can't believe I've been asleep that long.*

His drowsiness quickly faded when he looked up at the cell door. *Uh oh!* His eyes made contact with Reverend Wilson who was dressed in a bright red sweater and blue jeans. Wilson proceeded to walk through the open cell door and stand directly in front of Greg. Wilson stared down at Greg, giving him a stern look. "Sheriff, do you mind giving us some privacy?"

"Not at all, Reverend," Sims responded with a wide, sinister grin.

This isn't going to be good, Greg thought, rubbing his temples. His head pulsed in pain with every beat of his heart. Wilson didn't say a word but took a seat next to Greg on the small cot. After several seconds, Reverend Wilson caught Greg by surprise when he leaned over, put his arm around his shoulder, and slowly began patting him on the back.

In a soft low voice, he began to speak. "Greg, I think I owe you an apology."

Huh? Greg couldn't believe what he was hearing.

"I know I've been hard on you, but I've been thinking about what you said yesterday in my office, and I think you're right."

What? Greg turned his head and looked at his contrite gray-bearded boss, who continued to softly pat his back like a loving father. He began to wonder if he was still asleep and if this was merely a dream.

Wilson continued. "Greg, I heard about Rachel and I'm here to help. I know how much she means to you. I now see that I was wrong, and I want to help you find her."

Greg looked at Wilson face to face. "I don't know . . . where . . ." He began to get chocked up. Wilson continued to pat him on the back. "I don't know where she is," he finally managed to say as tears streamed down his face.

"Greg, I think that's where I can help."

"You know where she is? Is she okay?" Hope and joy began to surface in Greg's voice. His energy began build.

"Not exactly," Wilson stated, "but I've got a hunch."

"Where?" Greg asked, trying to stand on his wobbly legs. His stomach let out a loud growl and he winced in pain. Suddenly, he realized the source of his massive headache. He hadn't eaten in long time.

"Whoa," Wilson said as he quickly stood up to catch Greg in case he fell. "Let's get you outta here and get you something to eat."

After grabbing a quick bite at Dot's, Greg and Reverend Wilson jumped into Wilson's black Buick and headed out to find Rachel. Even though they ate quickly, Greg found the whole dining experience odd. In the fourteen months since he'd been back home, this was the first time they'd ever eaten together. Also, Wilson was unusually very talkative, overly friendly, and he kept asking Greg how he was feeling. Upon leaving the restaurant, Greg realized that Susie Price had forgotten to return his wallet and cell phone to him when he'd left the police station. Wilson paid for the meal and suggested they get going. Greg could get his personal belongings tomorrow.

No one said a word until they passed the two stone crosses at the edge of town. Greg began to grow suspicious. "So, uh . . . where're we going?"

"Greg, I know all about last October and what happened at the Lynch house. I know it's hard to understand, and I'm not saying that it's right, but folks here have always worried that if we talked about what happened in the past, it would somehow awaken the evil that they knew existed. I grew up in that culture; it's all I ever known."

"Reverend," Greg was about to speak as they turned onto County Road 10.

"Please, call me John."

Greg was having a hard time adjusting to his boss's new friendly disposition. "Uh, okay. John, I've never understood that way of thinking."

"In hindsight you're right, Greg; we should've done things differently. Ignoring problems is never the way to go.

I realize that now. I'm just sorry it took this situation to wake me up."

Greg looked down at his watch. It was 4:15, and the low-hanging sun indicated that dusk was right around the corner. "So, where you'd say we were going?"

"Greg, I'm going to need you to trust me. I'll explain everything later."

Trust you? Why should I, just because you're now being nice to me? Greg thought, looking at the vast acres of dark forest from beyond his passenger window. Then it occurred to him. *What choice do I have if I want to see Rachel again?* Greg was haunted by the last words Earl had spoken to him: "Greg, the Lord wants you to trust Him completely."

EIGHTEEN

Halfway down County Road 10, Greg noticed Wilson began to slow down. The narrow, two-lane road was deserted, as usual. With the sound of loose gravel being crushed underneath the tires, Wilson's car slowed to a crawl and finally eased off the road. Greg sat motionless with the palms of his hands on each leg. He instantly knew where they were going, and old fears began to well up inside him.

He immediately took a deep breath and let it out. Reverend Wilson reached over and, without saying a word, gave him a comforting pat on the arm. "We're going to the Lynch house, aren't we?" Greg asked, looking troubled.

"Yes," Wilson replied emphatically. He paused for a moment then continued. "Greg, I can't imagine how hard this must be for you, but like I said, I've got a hunch Rachel's here. I could be wrong."

Greg looked down at his watch; it was 4:35. Darkness was rapidly approaching. Long shadows stretched across the road and the pale white moon was already visible in the pre-twilight sky. "Why didn't we come sooner, it's almost dark?"

"Greg, I didn't get the call from Sheriff Sims until three o'clock this afternoon that you'd been arrested. I came to the police station as soon as I heard. Now we can sit here and argue while it continues to get darker or we can get going. I say we get going," Wilson replied.

Deep down Greg knew he was right; they were wasting precious daylight. "What if Loretta's there?" Greg asked, "How are we gonna protect ourselves?"

Wilson got out of the car, walked around to the back, and popped the trunk open. Greg got out of the passenger side and walked around to see the reverend holding a twelve-gauge shotgun with both hands. "I think this should do it," Wilson responded confidently. Greg knew otherwise, but at this point, all he wanted to do was find Rachel. He would trust the Lord with the rest.

Wilson slammed the trunk closed and both men began walking through the tall grass to the barbed-wire fence that separated the road from the woods. Each lifted the fence up for the other to slide through. It was another twenty yards from the fence to the edge of the woods.

Just approaching the woods brought bad memories that wreaked havoc on Greg's brain. He briefly reflected back to this exact day, one year ago—he and Cory carrying Earl, who was drenched in blood, all the way back to their truck. On the way back to town that night, Greg remembered thinking they'd looked as if they had survived a horrible car accident, instead of killing the town's vampire. This time, though, Earl and Cory weren't with him; he wished they were. He began to miss Earl, but the hope of finding Rachel, to hold her again, was pushing him past his fear.

Nighttime was coming fast. The forest seemed to be getting darker by the minute. Greg ducked under a couple of low-hanging branches and listened intently to the feet of deer scattering through the woods to his right. He could barely see Wilson, who was a good fifteen yards in front. *I can't believe we didn't bring flashlights,* Greg thought.

Greg picked up his pace to try to make up the ground between them. Sweat began to pour down his face and into his three-day-old beard. The sudden loud cry of a hawk echoed through the quiet, dense forest, causing him to jump, but he was determined to keep up his pace. He looked down at his watch. It was already past five o'clock, so he knew they had to be getting close. Never in a million years did he ever think he'd come back to the Lynch house, but yet here he was. *Lord, please help me find Rachel; please let her be okay,* he prayed in his head.

Finally, they made their way to the familiar opening in the woods. Only small hints of twilight remained as dusk settled upon the ruins of what use to be the Lynch house. Greg took a moment to look around trying to remember how the inside of the house looked. Bricks and half-burned debris lay spread across the foundation. Only the brick chimney remained intact. Based on his memory, Greg figured that he was probably standing just inside the front door in front of what used to be the winding staircase. He glanced to his right and saw the overgrown graveyard, which appeared untouched by the fire that had consumed the house a year ago. Through the weeds and brush, which was now waist high, he could see the two mounds of dirt under

PLAINRIDGE

the large oak tree. It was the very same dirt he, Earl, and Cory had moved this time last year when they were digging up the Lynch's graves.

"RACHEL!" Greg yelled at the top of his lungs, his voice echoing through the woods. Just a few feet in front of him, Wilson was walking around studying the ground. Standing in the remains of the burned house, Greg still felt a dark and sinister presence, the same presence he remembered feeling when he first saw the house.

Reverend Wilson now appeared focused on a certain area and had begun moving some bricks out of the way. At first, Greg wasn't sure what he was doing, and then it hit him. *He's found the cellar.* Greg walked over and stood next to Wilson. "Do you think Rachel's down there?" Greg asked.

Wilson was breathing heavy from moving the debris. "It's just a hunch, but I think this is where she would've taken her, if she's still alive that is."

Those last words struck him with such force, he thought he might pass out. He had to find her. Wilson got on one knee, cleared some more debris out of the way, and then grabbed the latch to the cellar door. With one pull he opened it up. A horrible smell arose from the cellar. Both men instinctively turned their heads away when they smelled the odor. With his hand covering his mouth and nose, Greg yelled down into the cellar. "RACHEL, ARE YOU DOWN THERE? CAN YOU HEAR ME?"

There was no response. "Greg, she may be unconscious. Let's go down there and check it out. It's

168

already dark; I'm not sure how much time we have left before Loretta shows up. I'll go first since I've got the shotgun."

With Wilson in front, both men slowly walked down the steps of the cellar. Greg continued praying in his mind, *Lord, please help me find her; please let her be okay.* Greg couldn't believe that one year later he was walking down the same flight of stairs that he had walked down a year ago. Evidently, the fire didn't reach the cellar.

The old, wooden stairs creaked loudly with each step they took. As they moved down, deeper into the earth, the overwhelming smell of death grew stronger. Greg knew that smell because he'd smelled it before; it was the unmistakable smell of decomposing bodies. It was obvious that she'd been here recently; he just hoped they weren't walking up on her now that it was dark.

Finally, they'd made their way down to the dirt floor of the cellar. It was pitch black. Greg was trying hard to adjust his eyes to the darkness. He'd lost Reverend Wilson. He could hear him walking around, but couldn't see him. Greg yelled Rachel's name again, "RACHEL!" There was no answer. "Reverend Wilson, where are you?" There was no answer. Greg could hear his footsteps. Like a blind man, with his hands stretched out in front of him, Greg began trying to feel his way around in the dark cellar. He tried to find a wall to give him some sort of bearing, something to hold on to. He tripped and stumbled on the uneven surface, but managed to keep from falling.

"Reverend, where are you?" Greg asked again, desperation in his voice. Again, there was no reply. This time, he didn't even hear any footsteps, just cold, empty silence. Greg felt fear exploding inside of him. He began to panic as he continued to feel his way through the darkness. His breathing began to accelerate. All he could hear was his own breathing and the sound of dirt moving when he shuffled his feet across the floor. Something wasn't right. *Why didn't the reverend answer me? Is Rachel down here? Is she unconscious, lying on the floor? Is Loretta standing back waiting on me?* Horrible thoughts raced through his mind. He continued to try to feel his way around the small, dark cellar. *BAM!*

***

Greg tried lifting his head upward. Through his blurred vision, he could see several flickers of light around the room. His head ached and he could feel the warm blood running down the back of his neck and into his shirt. He tried to move his arm, but couldn't. He didn't know what had happened or how long he'd been out, but the last thing he remembered was that he was trying to get out of the cellar, then nothing. He slowly opened his eyes again and to his horror, he realized he was still in the cellar. There were candles lit everywhere, providing a full view of the small room. The pungent smell of rotting flesh mixed with the moist, cool earth invaded his nostrils. Greg tried to move his arms again to cover his nose, but couldn't. He suddenly realized he was chained to the wall.

He lifted his head again when he heard the sound of footsteps coming his way. Even though his head continued to throb in pain, Greg's vision had improved and he was able to see the source of the horrible smell. In the corner to his left lay three partially decomposed bodies stacked on top of each other. He instantly recognized that one of the bodies was wearing a torn red Plainridge lacrosse jersey. Greg immediately vomited violently onto the dirt floor. Tears began to well up in his eyes. When he opened them again, Reverend Wilson was standing in front of him.

"I was beginning to wonder when you were going to wake up," Wilson stated rhetorically with his arms crossed.

"Why am I tied up?" Greg demanded, trying to jerk loose from the chains.

"Greg, I told you that I was familiar with what had happened here at the Lynch house last October, but what I didn't tell you was that I wasn't too happy about it. You see, Greg, unlike Sheriff Hayes, Mayor Watson, Jim Akin, and a few others, I had a different view of our town's secret history. Oh, those men knew it existed; they knew about the Lynch house and what happened here in October of 1858. They knew about Hester Lynch and the sacrifice that was owed every thirty to forty years, but they didn't embrace it like I did. They treated it, well . . . hmmm . . . how can I say this? They treated it like a bad storm that would come through every thirty to forty years. Their idea was to simply survive it and move on. They believed that if you talked about it openly, then that could somehow trigger it."

"Where's Rachel!" Greg demanded, interrupting Wilson.

"I'm not really sure, but she's probably not alive. Don't worry; you'll be reunited with her soon enough. Now back to what I was saying. Oh yes, Greg, back on October 31, 1858, our town made a covenant with the one true Lord—the god of this world—and he was faithful to us. My appointed work through the years was to honor that covenant and to make sure our town honored it. That's why I wasn't too happy when I learned that you and your friends killed Hester and Marlene Lynch and that Sheriff Hayes had burned down the house. You see, Greg, one thing John Hayes didn't fully understand is that you don't simply BREAK A COVENANT!" Wilson's angry red face became accentuated behind his white beard.

Tears rolled down Greg's face as he hung from the brick wall. He couldn't believe it was ending this way. Rachel was dead, Earl was dead, and he was about to be next. That was okay with him. Without Rachel, he didn't want to live anymore anyway. Wilson continued pacing in front of him, unaffected by his suffering. He continued. "So when I learned, through Jim Akin and Sheriff Hayes, that they'd buried Loretta in Asbury Cemetery, I was summoned to go and help her. I was the one who removed the dirt from her grave. That night, I waited for her to arise and when I saw her claws coming out of the earth, I knelt there in worship. Over the next year, I helped her survive in the shadows and inside my parish. Only recently did she begin to venture out on her own. I was the one who led her to John Hayes, Jim Akin, and the others for penance for what they had done. They had to pay. The town had to pay. Now Greg, it's your turn to pay."

At that moment, Greg heard a rustling of debris above them. Wilson looked up at the ceiling and closed his eyes. An ever so peaceful smile emerged across his face. "She's here, Greg. She's coming for you," Wilson stated, letting out an evil laugh that resonated throughout the room. His cold, black eyes stared at Greg, enjoying his torment. Greg raised his head toward the center of the room and the staircase. He watched in horror as Loretta slowly made her way down the steps. Her head and body twitched and contorted uncontrollably, but she was steady on her dirt-encrusted bare feet. Her filthy, ragged dress matched the dried blood and grime that stained her long fingernails. He wanted to scream, but couldn't. He found himself frozen in terror. Her face was hideously evil. He no longer recognized her as the woman he had known for years. Earl was right; this was evil personified. As she moved closer, the final words from Earl came to the forefront of his mind: *Greg, the Lord wants you to trust Him completely, no matter how bleak the situation seems.*

Fearing this was the end, Greg lowered his head and mumbled a short prayer. "Father, into Your hands I commend my spirit." Several seconds went by and nothing happened. Greg was afraid to raise his head; he didn't want to see her face again. *Why did she stop?* Finally, Greg looked up and at Loretta, who was ten feet from him, but she wasn't advancing. Instead, she took a step backwards with her head down as if she was somehow frightened by Greg. Just a couple of feet away, Wilson was on his knees worshipping her in adoration.

Then Greg remembered Earl's story on how he had encountered her at John Hayes' house and how he thought that it saw Jesus inside him. Even though he was physically chained to the wall, Greg felt himself becoming emboldened. His fear was fading. He began to speak to the evil spirit. "You have no authority over me, evil spirit; I belong to Jesus, the Son of the highest God. I COMMAND YOU TO LEAVE THIS PLACE NOW IN THE NAME OF JESUS!"

The demon turned its head and covered its face as if a magnificent light was radiating from Greg. Wilson, seeing what was happening, became visibly upset. "What are you doing?" Wilson screamed. "I brought him to you. As your servant, I've done everything you've asked of me."

The evil spirit lunged at Wilson, grabbing him by his throat. His screams rose from the depths of the cellar as Loretta feasted upon him. Greg recoiled and turned his head in disgust. Soon the screaming had stopped. Out of the corner of his eye, Greg could see his former boss's black boot twitch uncontrollably as Loretta continued to dine on his neck. Greg closed his eyes and began to pray. "Lord, please help me; I trust You."

The next sound he heard was a painful scream coming from Loretta. He looked up and saw an arrow sticking out of her back and through her chest. Then a sound of another arrow flying through the air and lodging into her chest. The evil spirit let out another loud scream before falling onto the dead reverend.

Greg looked to his left and saw Cory holding a crossbow; Mayor Watson was by his side. They both immediately rushed over and began removing the chains from Greg's arms.

"Greg, are you okay?" Cory asked, removing the chain from Greg's left hand. Greg immediately grabbed his dear friend and hugged him tight. Watson had made his way over to Loretta and was checking to make sure the arrow had gone through her heart. Greg continued to hold on to Cory.

"Greg, I've got great news. Rachel's fine. She's okay."

Greg turned loose of Cory and took a step back. Tears welled up in his eyes. He stumbled and almost collapsed but was caught by Cory's strong arms. "What did you say?

"I said she's fine. She's got a broken ankle, but other than that, she's fine. She's been trying to get in touch with you all day. She finally called me on my cell. She told me about what happened last night and how she was crawling down the sidewalk when she heard footsteps coming up behind her. She thought it was Loretta, but when she looked up, there was a large, bearded man with kind eyes standing over her. He gently picked her up and drove her to the hospital. That's all she remembers. After I hung up with her, I called Mayor Watson and he told me what had happened with you getting arrested early this morning. It was his idea to come up here."

Ed Watson turned around and looked at Greg and said, "I felt like the Lord was telling me that Wilson was bringing you back here. So, I called Cory and here we are. God is good."

"Yes He is!" Greg said, still holding on to Cory. "Is Rachel still at the hospital?"

"No, they released her this afternoon. Mrs. Watson picked her up. She's at home." Cory paused and smiled. "She's waiting on you. I promised her that I would bring you back to her."

EPILOGUE

TWO MONTHS LATER

Snow is a rare gift in the Deep South, especially in December. Rachel stood in her white wedding dress looking out the window at the majestic snow-covered scene before her. Behind her, a ten-foot Douglas fir with radiant white lights and various red and gold ornaments reflected back through the windowpane. She only wished her parents were alive to see her, to be here with her, for this special day. Just a few doors down, safely away from the bride, Greg and Cory stood next to each other in their matching black tuxedo's enjoying the beauty of the clean, white flakes falling from the gray winter sky.

It seemed like years ago since they were in that damp cellar at the Lynch house. Three weeks after Greg's rescue, he found himself on the front steps of the church, boldly preaching to the town's two thousand residents. Quoting from Joshua chapter 24 verse 15, Greg challenged the crowd on that cold, gray November afternoon. "If you decide that it's a bad thing to worship God, then choose a god you'd rather serve—and do it today. Choose one of the gods your grandparents worshiped, but as for me and my family, we'll worship the Lord." When he had concluded his sermon, there was an altar call and the vast majority of the people in town received Jesus as their Lord and Savior. After the service, Greg, Cory, and Ed Watson conducted a baptism service for all those who had received Christ. The baptism service went on for six straight hours until the last person was baptized.

Three weeks later, Mayor Ed Watson introduced a bill before the newly elected city council, calling for the name of the town to be officially changed back to Crossville. The new bill also included a proposed new town charter, in which the town of Crossville, Alabama, would once again be dedicated to the Lord. The bill was passed unanimously and was signed into law the very next day.

On the same day that the new bill was signed into law, a strange and unexplainable event occurred at the former Lynch house. Apparently, according to the Montgomery Fire and Rescue Department, there was a random lightning strike that hit directly where the Lynch house was formerly located, starting a massive wildfire. Firefighters from the surrounding areas were brought in to try to help contain the fire. According to many of the firefighters, the heat from the fire was so hot that they were unable to approach the forest. Fortunately, after two days, an unexpected low-pressure center suddenly developed, dumping massive amounts of rain on the middle part of the state, thus quenching the fire.

Dan Blevins, a thirty-five-year veteran of the Montgomery Fire Department said that in his entire time as a firefighter, he'd never seen a fire as hot as the one they encountered off County Road 10. Furthermore, he stated, "This is the first time in my life I've seen a lighting strike occur on a clear and sunny afternoon."

Greg took a deep breath and exhaled as he waited for his bride. He casually turned around and barely made eye contact with his best man, Cory, who returned his stare with a smile and reassuring pat on the back. Then moments later, the church organ cranked up. Everyone in the church stood up and turned their heads back toward the front doors.

Then on cue, the two Anglican-style wooden front doors of the church gently opened, simultaneously, revealing the snow-covered yard and steps. Then around the corner came the most beautiful thing Greg had ever seen. A lump crested in his throat when he saw her. Her white dress, blending in with the snow and her long, jet-black hair flowing down her dress, looked like a scene out of a fairy tale. This was her moment. She continued her march down the aisle, escorted by Ed Watson, who had a huge smile across his face. Greg took it all in, enjoying every second. When they reached the church altar, Watson reached out and shook Greg's hand. Rachel grabbed Greg's arm tightly and turned toward the town's new reverend, who proceeded with, "Dearly beloved, we are gathered here today, before almighty God."

On the surface, Plainridge appears to be an ordinary small, Southern town. However, to a few of the locals, the town has a dark past, which has been kept a secret.

Greg Jones reluctantly moves back to his hometown after college. Not long after moving back, he begins to discover the town's evil secret as well as his own destiny.

About the Author

Steve Stratton, the author of *One October* and *Plainridge*, received his degree in Business Administration from the University of Alabama and currently works in the banking industry. When he is not writing, he enjoys spending time with his family. Steve currently resides in Huntsville, Alabama.

CPSIA information can be obtained at www.ICGtesting.com
Printed in the USA
LVOW13s1753260913

354244LV00002B/5/P

9 781613 141700